Sabotage in the Sails

A Nora Jones Mystery

Heather Huffman

Edited by Justin LaMonda

Cover Design by Madhat Studios

For Blake. I've never known someone more able to make people smile.
You're smart, funny & kind—and so much of who I wish I was.
Love you always.

Chapter One

NORA JONES FURROWED HER brow, mentally repeating the steps in her head as Rafael called out, "Ready to tack?"

She took a deep breath before replying, "Ready." Nora hoped she meant it. She had nightmares about losing control of the boom and knocking Rafael out because she mixed up some sailboat terminology or hit the wind at the wrong angle. From a distance, sailing looked so serene. Up close, it was something of a ballet between the crew, the wind, the sea, and the boat. There was an art to understanding how to maneuver the opposing forces of the wind and sea to propel your craft forward.

Nora was beginning to realize that when it was you holding the ropes and responsible for the boat doing all of the things, it was incredibly intimidating.

"Tacking!" Rafael called out once the boat had built up enough speed, ending Nora's musings as she scurried to release the line controlling the jib on the starboard side and grab the portside line. She couldn't be sure if she was reciting the steps in her head or out loud, but before long, the sails caught the wind from the starboard side, and she was securing the jib sheet portside.

"Pull the jib sheet in just a tiny bit so we're close hauled," he instructed.

Nora hurried to comply, biting her lip in thought as she untied her knot, adjusted the line, and resecured it. She looked up expectantly when that was accomplished.

Rafael raised a quizzical eyebrow, causing Nora to catch her breath, her mind racing to sort out what she'd done wrong before he broke into a grin. "Nicely done, my love."

"Really?" She brightened.

"Absolutely," he reassured her. "You're a natural."

Inordinately pleased, Nora stood and wrapped her arms around Rafael's waist, contenting herself to relish in the victory of the moment, the rocking of the boat beneath their feet, and the feel of the wind as they sliced through it. It hadn't been that long ago she'd still been grumbling about why they couldn't just say right and left instead of starboard and port. She'd come a long way since she and Raf had begun their lessons. He still wanted to teach her to scuba dive, but she'd been much more interested in sailing. Something about being on the *Magnolia Jane* made her feel closer to her Uncle Walter—and even to his friend Lucca Buccio, the retired mob boss who had become Nora's unlikely champion.

Eventually, she wanted to get Margo out on the boat with her. But the greyhound was so unpredictable when it came to new situations that Nora had opted to wait until she was surer of herself to add another dynamic. It seemed the prudent thing to do for everyone's safety. They stayed on the water a bit longer before calling it a day. Nora would have been more inclined to stay and watch the sunset if she wasn't already missing Margo so fiercely.

Besides, they had an appointment with Pru before dinner. After months of trying to get it scheduled, their friend had finally gotten her wish to paint Nora and Rafael. Well, their voices, anyway. Chromesthesia allowed Prudence to see visual displays whenever she heard sound, a neurological anomaly that would have left Nora seeking a fortress of solitude to get away from the sensory overload. Nora thought her astigmatism made driving at night wholly overwhelming. She couldn't imagine seeing a Pink Floyd light show with every sound.

But Pru was made of sterner stuff than that and harnessed her unique ability to see sound into a new way to create art, turning everything from a Mozart concerto to the most mundane of conversations into stunning paintings. Though they were both fans of Pru's work, this was the first time Nora and Raf had sat for a session.

"What color do you think I am?" Rafael mused.

"Twilight blue," Nora answered.

"Really? Why blue?" he wondered.

Nora considered trying to convince him she just had a sense for these things, but instead admitted, "Pru told me."

Rafael cracked a grin in response. "You were debating whether or not to be honest about that, weren't you?"

"Absolutely," she replied.

It didn't take long for them to return to the dock. As pleasant as the outing had been, Nora couldn't help noticing Rafael had something on his mind, no matter how much he insisted otherwise. She tried not to pry—she wanted them to be the kind of couple that gave each other space and trust—but she had to admit it was eating at her not knowing what was going through his head, even if just the teensiest bit.

Her suspicion was furthered when Rafael uncharacteristically let her tie the boat up alone while he scowled at the text he was answering. When she was done, she came to stand at his side, her expression curious as she waited for him to finish. He glanced up and forced a smile.

"Work stuff," was the only explanation she received before he planted a kiss on her cheek and hopped off the boat and onto the dock. Perhaps it was childish, but Nora found herself silently mimicking "work stuff" behind his back before clambering out of the boat as well.

However irritated she was with Rafael, it dissipated when they bumped into a neatly dressed older man as they crossed the parking lot. She didn't know his name, though she'd seen him around the marina a few times. Nora instinctively pressed in closer to Raf as they passed. He didn't need to know the story to sense what she needed, wrapping his arm around her waist in response. Not that Nora could have explained her reaction if she tried. There was just something about the way that man looked at her that made her stomach tighten. As so many women do, Nora had learned young not to ignore it when her stomach tightened in a bad way around a man.

In the car, she did her best to shake off the odd encounter. She'd been looking forward to seeing these paintings for months. Pru had actually done two paintings from their session—one while they were in person and the second from a recording of the conversation, just to see what differences there would be between the two. It was an experiment Nora had been happy to participate in. Her favorite painting to date was one Pru had done of their friends August and Leo having a conversation about what to have for dinner. It reminded Nora that there is beauty in the ordinary.

Rafael seemed to be lost in thought and Nora found herself musing that she was glad traffic wasn't awful. There were many reasons she loved her new home, but the traffic during tourist season was not among them. It's possible she also spent part of the ride trying to figure out what was wrong with Raf, but only part of it. Ultimately, he was a grownup. He'd either tell her or he wouldn't. Either way, she was determined not to let his decision dictate how much she enjoyed her day.

She'd managed to tack the boat all by herself—and dock it—and they were on their way to pick up their very own Prudence Willoughby original. There was no need to allow a cloud over her mood on a day with so many victories.

It didn't take long to navigate over to Pru's cozy little gallery over on King Street, Sound Art. When the gallery her friend worked at had shut down, Nora had been prepared to buy it for her since she felt at least partly responsible for the place's demise. As it turns out, getting a store's owners arrested was bad for business. But Pru had insisted her studio was more than enough space for her vision, so she'd turned it into a storefront as well as an art studio, ordered a sign for the front door, and declared herself open for business.

Having chromesthesia had turned her into enough of a recluse that she'd been saving money for years, not even really knowing what for. After meeting with Ivy—their friend group's resident "money person"—Pru was confident she had the means to sustain herself while she got her little gallery off the ground. Nora, for one, couldn't wait to see what she did with it.

"There you are!" The tiny blonde greeted them with a bright smile as the couple entered the shop.

"I tacked the boat all by myself. And I took it back to the marina alone, too," Nora proudly informed her friend.

"I'm not sure I know what that means, but yay!"

"It means Nora is becoming quite the sailor," Rafael explained, pulling Nora affectionately to his side and kissing her temple.

Nora wasn't sure what to make of the praise in light of his mood swings, so she changed the subject. "Are you rearranging?"

Pru cast a glance around the studio, which was now half-empty. "I had to make room for my new tenant."

"New tenant? Do tell." Nora was all ears.

"Ivy finally convinced her brother to move here. He's an artist and she thought it would make sense for both of us to share the space. It'll give me a buffer in my budget—and he doesn't mind people, so he said he'd teach classes a couple nights a week if I'd manage the office stuff."

"Nice." Nora felt a bit like a bad friend for not realizing Ivy had a brother, but she set it aside to focus on Pru's news. "When does he get here?"

"By the end of the week. He seems pretty cool, but we've only emailed, so I'm a little nervous."

"That's understandable," Nora commiserated. "But Ivy knows you both pretty well. She must think it's a good fit or she wouldn't have suggested it."

"Here's hoping."

"So, where's the paintings I've heard so much about?" Rafael asked. Even though his voice was pleasant, Nora couldn't help wondering if he was eager to get out of there to deal with whatever was causing his phone to vibrate periodically.

"Oh, right! They're back here." Pru motioned for them to follow her as she headed toward the back of the studio. She came to a stop in front of two similar paintings sitting side-by-side. One seemed more muted than the other, with slightly more subdued tones and less depth to the brushstrokes, but otherwise, they were nearly identical.

"Wow." Nora soaked it in, leaning forward to study them more closely. Given the deep blue of Rafael's voice, she was surprised by Pru's decision to place the swirls on a black backdrop, but the interplay of the darker colors with the sunny blue of Nora's own voice and the shimmers of light interplaying throughout gave the entire thing an ethereal quality. "Our voices are so pretty together."

"They really are," Rafael agreed, reaching out to not quite touch the canvas with his fingers as he traced the path of the swirls. Two different shades of blue danced around each other, one bright and vibrant, one rich and velvety. "Sometimes I envy the world you experience."

"Thank you." Pru seemed touched by his words, making Nora wonder if anyone had ever complimented her chromesthesia before. "The one here on the left was from the in person conversation. The one on the right is from the recording. I tried to space it a few days apart so I wouldn't be too heavily influenced by my memory of the first conversation."

"Smart," Nora commented. "It's amazing how similar they are."

"And interesting that the recorded conversation is more muted," Rafael added. "Though not entirely surprising."

"It's fuzzier, too." Nora studied the painting. "And is there a hint of pink in this one?"

"There is." Rafael joined her in examining them more closely. "I wonder if it was static or feedback from the recording. Either way, this is amazing, Pru. Thank you."

"Now we just have to figure out who gets which painting." Nora straightened.

Rafael shook his head. "My place is a tiny bachelor pad. They should both go to your house. We can figure out where to hang them this weekend if you want."

"It's a date." Nora had to agree with his assessment. She could count on one hand the number of times she'd seen his apartment since they'd begun dating. It was small, clean, and sparsely decorated. It felt more like a stopping-off point than a home, in Nora's opinion.

They visited with Pru a moment more, lingering to admire some of her newer work and talk about her plans for the place before heading out. Rafael dropped Nora at her house, tucking the paintings into an out-of-the-way corner where they would be safe until they could be hung. After he'd gone, Nora headed over to Raymond's to pick up Margo. The retired greyhound was delighted to see her person, even though Nora was certain the dog had been spoiled rotten by Raymond in her absence. Still, the leaps and twirls from Margo warmed Nora's heart. Everyone needed someone who adored them so fully.

"Nora, my dear." Raymond greeted her with a kiss on the cheek once the dog had settled enough for him to get close. "How did sailing go?"

"Really well! I'm getting better every day. There's so much to remember, though." Nora stepped inside the house.

"Want a glass of wine? I'd love to hear about your day."

Nora was tired, but it was rare that Raymond invited her to stay. She suspected he was grappling with a wave of loneliness, so she accepted, settling in a seat while she waited for him to pour her a glass of sparkling wine.

"It would make Walter happy to know the *Magnolia Jane* is with you. He loved that boat."

"It seems like it was special to both him and to Lucca."

Raymond nodded, taking a sip of his wine before responding. "Yes, well, they restored her together."

"Did they?" Nora perked up, always eager for another kernel of knowledge about her uncle.

"She came from a government auction site. Her owner had been neglecting to pay his taxes, I believe. She'd rather fallen into disrepair, so they snapped her up at a steal. Cleaned her up and taught themselves to sail."

"I guess I didn't realize that *Janey* came before *Amelia*," Nora mused. "I'd always assumed he'd used the money from their findings to buy her."

"I only knew Walter tangentially back then, but I got the impression that it was while they were working on the *Magnolia Jane* that the idea to become treasure hunters was born."

"Interesting." Nora mulled over his words. "I never realized."

In fact, Nora had been learning about her long-lost uncle in bits and bobs for nearly a year and she was convinced she'd never know the full picture. Even the most mundane among us has secrets, and Walter Cavanaugh had been anything but mundane.

Chapter Two

IT WAS A BEAUTIFUL day, though a hot one. Being a Northern California girl most of her life, the heat of a Florida summer was taking some adjusting to for Nora. Margo, a Florida girl through and through, was completely nonplussed by the muggy air as she entreated Nora to throw the ball one more time.

"This is the last one," Nora informed the dog. "We have to open the shop up for Courtney and then August is expecting us at the farm." Perhaps "farm" wasn't the most accurate description for the animal sanctuary August ran for Nora, but somehow, they'd all started calling it that.

Margo was not impressed by schedules or obligations, rather dropping the ball at Nora's feet, looking from the toy to her person and back again, expectation written plainly on her face.

"Nice try, my love. But we really do have to go." As she rounded up Margo's bag for the day and got the dog fastened into her seat, Nora couldn't help wondering if this was what it was like having to get a child out the door. She couldn't begin to imagine having to get multiple little humans in the car. Whenever thoughts that like surfaced, she became even more comfortable with her decision to remain Aunt Nora, spoiling Charlotte and the legion of siblings she'd one day have.

On their way to the bookshop, Nora and Margo popped by the neighbor's bakery to pick up breakfast. As much as the cinnamon rolls Mykal just pulled out of the oven were calling her name, Nora was aware that Courtney paid attention to every bite of food she ate, so she picked up a spinach and red pepper frittata instead.

Not long after being hired, the other woman had told Nora that she had PCOS, which—among other things—made the pounds cling stubbornly to her no matter how carefully she ate or how active she was.

"But I find that I enjoy life more if I stick to my PCOS-friendly diet and exercise," Courtney had said.

Nora found it admirable, though she did have to wonder at a society that made a woman beyond a certain size feel compelled to explain themselves. Nora never felt the need to explain her brown eyes or the decided lack of curl in her hair.

After exchanging pleasantries with Mykal, Nora headed over to the shop, where Margo waited patiently for Nora to find her keys and open the door. Someday, Nora would think to fish her keys out of her bag before leaving the bakery. This was not that day.

Finally triumphant, Nora let them into the little store, setting breakfast on the counter before going about her morning routine. She still wasn't used to it, the newfound quiet. When August had left to take over Quirkiosities, the name they'd dubbed their sanctuary for misfit animals, Leo had set up his studio in one of the vacant cabins on the property. Nora was happy to reclaim the upstairs at the shop but also a little sad to see him go. The couple had a warm, happy energy to them that she missed.

Their departure had come right on the heels of Pru leaving to pursue her dream of being an artist. Logically, Nora knew that they'd been gone three months, and she'd only owned the shop for nine, but she still missed them. Of course, it was hard to believe she hadn't even been here a full year. So much had happened in such a short time. Her life before felt as distant as another universe.

"Good morning!" Courtney greeted her brightly, pulling Nora out of her reverie.

Nora smiled and returned the greeting. Courtney had hair that was somewhere between brown and blonde; she kept it pulled back in a loose barrette, so it tumbled down her back in long, soft curls. With a round face and a soft smile that was always at the ready, Courtney was, at a glance, a warm and kind woman. But, if you listened, it soon became apparent that she also had a keen sense of observation and a wit that could bite. No wonder August had hired her on the spot after a single interview.

Nora listened with one ear as Courtney filled her in on her date the night before. She couldn't help thinking of these morning recaps as her daily soap opera. If Courtney's experience with dating apps were indicative of what was truly out there, then Nora might swear off men altogether if things didn't work out with Raf.

For the first time since they'd started dating, it occurred to Nora that things might not work out with Rafael. It wasn't a thought that sat comfortably with her, so she set it aside and refocused her attention on Courtney's harrowing journey into work that morning, the conversation having moved on from the date who wasn't over his ex.

"It's always men in white trucks, have you noticed that?"

Nora raised her eyebrows, wondering what was always men in white trucks.

"The rude ones," Courtney explained. "Someone bullies you on the road, it's usually a man in a white truck."

"I don't believe I've noticed that, but I'll have to pay closer attention."

"And if they have testicles hanging from the back of that white truck, it's pretty much a given they have little man syndrome, so it's best just to stay out of their way."

"So, testicles hanging from the truck equates a Napoleon complex?" Nora tried to follow along.

"No, I mean little *man.*" Courtney shook her head and stuck out her pinky. "I figure if they have to publicly assure you that they have all their parts, then something's not right down there."

Nora choked on the bite of frittata she'd just taken. "Solid reasoning," she agreed when she'd composed herself. Inwardly, she hoped Courtney didn't share those theories with their customers.

The conversation resurfaced in her mind as she loaded Margo up for their drive to Quirkiosities later that day. As she navigated her way from the historic district to the highway, her personal observation was that all the cars were equally rude. The general impatience that permeated society was amplified behind the wheel of a car.

Nora had come to see her drives out to the farm as her time to think. It was a welcome escape from the constant traffic of town now that tourist season was upon them, and the miles always rolled by too quickly. The scenery changed from palm trees and sand to towering oaks, lush green sod farms, and row after row of potatoes and cabbage.

After buying the farm, Nora did some research and realized that Federal Point had a rich history of its own, both for the Native American tribes that once inhabited it and as the breadbasket for St. Augustine, thanks to its location on the St. John's River.

She turned down the long, tree-lined drive, eager to see her friends and to spend a day in the sunshine, even if it meant August would work her until her legs were gelatinous. Before she emerged into the parking area, Nora was greeted by Buck, the half-Corgi/half-Great Pyrenees dog who'd appointed himself guardian of the realm. He ran alongside the car barking, his tail in the air like a banner heralding their arrival.

Thankfully, he'd come to accept Nora and Margo as part of his pack, so they were allowed out of the car when they parked. Not all who ventured down the driveway were so lucky. Just last week, Nora had gotten a call from a contractor who was trapped in his truck by the squat tank of a dog. She wondered how that would work when the place opened to visitors, which was the ultimate goal. For some reason, Ivy was rather insistent that the businesses Nora kept buying eventually needed to start turning a profit. Chief Financial Officers were weird like that.

Nora got Margo out of the car, releasing her leash and giving the dog verbal permission to go play. The words were barely out of her mouth before Margo was off like a shot, her long legs hardly touching the ground as she zoomed every which direction. Despite his distinct lack of leg length, Buck tried valiantly to keep up. In the distance, she could hear Ol' Jack barking. Nora wondered if the ancient dog was cheering them on, scolding them, or just standing in a corner confused somewhere. All were equally possible.

There were very few places Nora felt comfortable letting Margo off-lead, so the first thing she'd done when buying the property was invest in a good fence around the perimeter. Even if Margo did get distracted by a squirrel and forget her recall training, she couldn't get far enough to get herself into too much trouble. The dog's desire to stay close to Nora meant she never wandered far, though. The fence was just a precaution because Nora had heard horror stories about greyhounds getting themselves lost because they'd taken off after something that captured their interest.

Nora's attention was pulled away from the dogs when August greeted her wearing a pair of jeans and a t-shirt that read, "Hold on, let me overthink this." Nora couldn't help observing that her friend had traded boho skirts for jeans since moving in at the farm, a transition that probably had more to do with practicality than fashion. August was an odd mix of free-spirited and practical, two traits Nora didn't often associate with each other.

Their greetings were interrupted by a sun-kissed, dirt-covered little girl whose curls stubbornly escaped their ribbons to fly free as she raced toward them as fast as her five-year-old legs would carry her.

"Auntie Nora!" The child flew at Nora with enough force to send her a step back, wrapping her arms around Nora's neck when she knelt for a hug.

"Charlotte, love. I have missed you. How's life on the farm?"

"I got to help Leo feed the snakes!"

"Nice. That sounds... terrifying."

"The snake grabbed the mouse like this—" Charlotte demonstrated with a quick grabbing motion, her eyes looking up at Nora to see if she was duly impressed.

"Wow. That's super-fast."

"It scared Leo." Charlotte giggled. "He said 'oh sh—'"

"We don't need to finish that story." August interrupted before her daughter could finish the word. "And I've told you never to repeat what Leo says when he feeds the snakes."

Charlotte's giggle deepened, clearly delighted with the reaction she got from her mother.

"You are such an imp." August's accusation held great affection. She tussled the girl's already riotous hair and smile. "How about we show Auntie Nora everything we've accomplished since she was here last time?"

Charlotte nodded enthusiastically, grabbing Nora's hand without preamble and dragging her along. Nora was pleased to see that construction on Zelda's enclosure had been completed. The bear was no longer in a cage, but rather sprawled out on a picnic table, soaking up the morning sun.

"You gave her a picnic table?" A grin tugged at Nora's lips.

August shrugged. "It seemed fitting. She likes it. She gets sun in the morning and shade in the afternoon. She has lots of toys and trees, but the picnic table is her favorite thing."

Next came Lilith, the one-eyed sloth. She appeared to be winking at them as she hung upside down from her tree branch long enough to snag a flower off a nearby hibiscus and shove it in her mouth.

"She really likes hibiscus," August explained. "And zucchini."

"Then we have that in common," Nora replied, pausing to watch the animal clamber back to her hammock.

They came up to an empty enclosure that had what looked to be the beginnings of a pond in the middle.

"Is this Ferdinand's upgrade?" Nora asked.

"It is." August beamed. "I want him to be a centerpiece. Pru is gathering a crew of artists to come paint the concrete fencing, so he'll have his own little art gallery."

"You do know someone put him in the gallery; he's not really an afficionado, right?" Nora pointed out, nonetheless amused by the enclosure August was having built for him.

"Nah, he has an appreciation for the finer things. I can tell."

Not one to argue with that logic, Nora smiled and asked what her assignment for the day was. August might seem all boho and fun, but she could be quite the taskmaster when the occasion arose, and this turned out to be such an occasion. By the time Nora sank back into her car hours later, her muscles felt like mush, her hair had sticks in it, and she'd broken not one but two nails. And she was pretty sure she was developing a nasty case of poison something-or-other. But she'd successfully cleared her assigned patch of land so the construction crew could start on the increased liger enclosure on Monday.

Some part of Nora wondered what was the point of being a millionaire if she couldn't afford to pay someone to clear the land for her, but August had already explained that starting with a clean slate was the only way she could get her construction bid low enough for Ivy to approve it. Nora was smart enough to trust the experts she'd surrounded herself with, and if Ivy had them on a budget, they'd best stick to it. Too many people depended on Nora for a paycheck at this point for her to fritter her money away on frivolous things like not wanting her muscles to feel like goo or to ruin a perfectly good manicure.

August had invited Nora to stay for dinner; Leo was throwing veggie kabobs on the grill. As much as she wanted to stay and enjoy her friends—and Leo's cooking—she wanted her pajamas more, so she'd rounded up an equally tired Margo and the pair had headed home.

Few things had ever felt as good to Nora as her shower did that night. She lingered even after she was done rinsing her hair, just letting the warmth of the water soothe her aching muscles. When she was finished, she wrapped up in her favorite robe and padded down to the kitchen to pour herself a glass of pinot grigio and scavenge dinner.

She'd barely finished her salad when her phone vibrated, signaling she'd gotten a text. She frowned as she read the somewhat clipped note from Rafael canceling their plans to go sailing later in the week. He wasn't acting like himself at all recently, and it was giving her an uneasy feeling. Was she about to be dumped? She'd been with Aaron for years. After his death, she'd spent even more years mourning his loss. So, it had been a hot minute since Nora had been dumped, but the way Raf was distancing himself made the warning bells go off in her head.

Even as she texted him that she understood—she didn't—she rationalized to herself that all relationships hit a certain point where they either progressed or fizzled. Certainly, everyone expected them to get married someday, including Nora. She'd assumed Raf hadn't proposed because he was respecting the fact that Nora had wanted to take things slowly. They hadn't even been together for a year, but maybe it was fizzle time already.

Suddenly more tired than hungry, Nora put the rest of her meal back in the fridge and walked Margo before trudging up the stairs to melt into her bed.

The next morning, she awoke with a renewed sense of purpose. She also had a body full of aching muscles that protested when she climbed out of bed, but she was as determined to ignore them as she was to not allow Rafael's moods to keep her from embracing life fully. The *Magnolia Jane* was a small enough rig for one person to handle. There was no reason she couldn't go sailing this week if she stayed in the bay, where it was safer.

With that decided, she dressed for work in a snappy blue and white sailor-inspired outfit. She fixed her hair and did her best to repair the damage to her nails and felt, in all, pretty good about herself by the time she chose Margo's collar and leash for the day.

On her way to the bookshop, she stopped at Mykal's bakery to grab breakfast for her crew and a cold brew coffee for herself.

"Good morning, Nora," Mykal's mother called out from behind the cash register.

"Good morning, Terra!" Nora replied with more cheer than she felt.

"You and Margo are both looking very sharp in your sailor suits," Terra commented.

"Why, thank you." Somewhere in the past year, Nora had become the kind of woman who dressed her dog in matching outfits. Well, more often the dog's collar and leash coordinated with Nora's outfit for the day. But truth be told, sometimes Margo got her own outfit, too. Today, the fawn-colored dog was sporting a blue collar and leash that were dotted with little white anchors. She also had on a white sailor hat that Nora was honestly shocked Margo had left in place this long. She fully expected her to wriggle out of it before the morning was through.

"I thought I heard you two out here." Mykal emerged from the kitchen. "Love the outfits."

"Good morning," Nora replied brightly. "And thank you. We're sailors now, you know. Well, I am. I'm still waiting until I'm a bit more confident to take Margo with me."

"I have always wanted to go sailing." Mykal's voice was wistful.

Nora didn't hesitate in extending an offer. "You should come with me some time. It would be nice to have a sailing buddy."

"I thought you and Rafael had been going together," Terra said.

Nora frowned. "We have, but he seems to be losing interest."

"I'd like that," Mykal answered the initial invitation.

"Wonderful! I was planning to go out later this week if you want. I'll text you later so we can work out the details."

Mykal smiled at her. "Sounds like a plan."

It made Nora happy that she and Mykal were becoming friends. After their rocky start, she hadn't been sure they'd make it this far, but Mykal's father was very dear to Nora, and she'd been determined to heal the rift between them for Lucca's sake, if nothing else. When she left the little shop, her arms were loaded down with goodies and her heart was much lighter than it had been upon entering.

Chapter Three

THE DAY NORA AND Mykal set out on their sailing adventure promised to be a glorious one. The sky was bright and beautiful, and there was just enough breeze to keep them skimming along the water nicely without Nora having to wrestle the sails too terribly much. There was something exhilarating about being the one responsible for whether or not the boat moved—and moved in the right direction. It was the first real test of her abilities, and Nora was pleased to think she was passing.

Nora secured her jib sheet and settled into her seat, content to soak in the sun now that their course was set. After skimming the ocean around them, hoping to spot some dolphins or something, her eyes landed on Mykal. In so many ways, the petite woman was a replica of her mother—the shy smile, the long mahogany hair, the heart-shaped face. But she had her father's dark eyes and there was something in her mannerisms that made her think of Lucca Buccio. Think of him and miss him, however unlikely their friendship might have been.

"You know," Nora began, "I recently found out that restoring this boat is what brought your father and my uncle together."

"Really?"

Mykal seemed genuinely interested, so Nora continued. "Yeah. I always assumed they bought the boat with their treasure haul, but Raymond says the boat is what inspired them to go on a treasure hunt."

"Kind of makes you wonder how such an unlikely pair came to buy a boat together in Florida, though, doesn't it?"

"Last time I asked, Lucca told me it was a story for another day." Nora gave herself a moment to get lost in a memory. It felt like a lifetime ago that she'd been sitting in Lucca's car, half fascinated and half terrified—and wholly certain Rafael would be furious with her when he'd found out.

"Let me guess, that day never came?" Mykal accurately surmised.

"It did not," Nora confirmed.

"Typical." Mykal rolled her eyes and leaned back, tilting her face up to the sun. "Those guys are always so cryptic."

"My experience with the mob is rather limited—though not as limited as Rafael would prefer it to be," Nora amended. "But you aren't wrong."

Mykal looked like she wanted to say more but held her tongue. Given the start to their relationship, Nora had no intention of prying, even if she was curious to know what the expression meant.

"How are things going with Rafael?"

Nora considered before answering honestly. "Not great, really. He's been sort of off lately."

"Another woman?"

"No." Nora paused, putting some thought to her reflexive answer before continuing. "No, I really don't think so. But he's got something on his mind. He seems to be pulling away."

"When Edmund started that, it was work."

"I don't think I've heard about Edmund."

Mykal shrugged. "Just an ex."

"Ah. Well, maybe. But I worry it's because things haven't progressed. We've been together for a while now and we're still about where we were six months ago. Is that bad?"

"I guess it depends on where you were six months ago."

"Shouldn't the relationship be moving toward something?" Nora wondered.

"I don't know—should it? Can't a good relationship just exist? Does it have to have an end goal?"

Nora turned the notion idea over in her mind, as if examining some foreign object. "Don't let my mother or his grandmother hear that. They'll have apoplexy. They're chomping at the bit for grandbabies."

"Maybe they should volunteer at a NICU or something, then. To be a baby cuddler."

"That's a thing?"

Mykal nodded. "It is."

"Huh. Not sure they'd see it as quite the same, but I'll suggest it sometime if I'm feeling particularly brave."

A brief grin tugged the corner of Mykal's mouth before she returned to the original topic at hand. "Maybe Rafael has the baby bug as bad as his grandmother, but I doubt it. He doesn't strike me as the type. My vote is work. Something's going down there that's got his attention."

"You're probably right." Nora wasn't sure how this newfound insight would help. It was highly unlikely she'd get Raf to open up to her about anything going on at the office. He'd be too afraid she'd meddle or something. "I want to hear about Edmund."

Mykal let out of bark of laughter. "You are like a dog with a bone, Nora."

"So I've been told."

"There's not much to tell. He was too good looking and too much trouble with a capital T."

"Those are fun." Nora found herself sighing wistfully before she caught herself. "Or so I've heard."

"What's this? Did I just catch a glimpse of the naughty side of Nora Jones?" Mykal teased, earning a blush from Nora.

"How's business?" Nora steered the conversation in a safer direction.

Mykal's expression said the change of topics amused her, but she let it pass without comment. "You know, pretty good. I think locals are starting to forgive us for taking over the smoothie shop. Starting to trust we're not going to slip them antifreeze in their drinks, anyway."

"Always a plus," Nora interjected.

"It really is," Mykal agreed. "And now that we're in tourist season, things are golden. I really expected it to take longer for us to take off, so I'm pretty happy."

"Good. Although don't get too popular. My staff will revolt if I don't bring them something from your shop every morning. I think Pru misses your quiche more than she does working for me."

"It is good quiche."

"So good." Nora agreed as she eyed their surroundings. They were heading further out than she'd intended; conversation had just been so enjoyable that she'd let them stay the course a little long. But now the wind was picking up, and they would soon be in open water. There was only one other boat nearby, and it, too, was veering back toward the marina. "I guess I should turn us around."

"Need any help?"

"Just watch your head. This boom will swing across the boat here in a second, and I don't want you to get whacked by it."

"Stay out of the way? I can do that!" Mykal moved out of striking distance. As she got settled, Nora ran through her mental checklist.

"Tacking!" She called out once she was ready. Just as she'd done before, she released the starboard jib sheet and grabbed the portside jib sheet, relishing the feel of the double-braided rope in her hands. There was a satisfying tug as the sails caught the wind from the starboard side without a hitch, and she was soon securing the jib sheet portside, tying the bowline just as Rafael taught her. She was about to sit back down when one last look at the sails made her question if they were in quite the right position. She'd just begun to pull the jib sheet in a bit more when there was a crack and the boom swung loose, the heavy wooden beam knocking Nora backward off the boat as it sliced through the air. She clawed her way to the surface, sputtering and trying to keep her head above water that felt much choppier now that she was in it. Nora's frantic brain tried to process the shadow over her, and she glanced up just in time to see the mast and sails tumbling toward her before she felt a sharp pain and the world went black.

"Can't you run it through the mass spectrometer or something?"

Nora was aware of August's voice, but the question didn't make any sense. She struggled to open her eyes. The effort of it all hurt too much, so she just listened, hoping to sort out what was going on.

"Run what through the what?" Rafael asked.

Leo interrupted before August could answer. "Sweetheart, you have got to stop watching *Bones.*"

"It's nostalgic. Have you seen the state of things? I need nostalgia right now."

"I suppose it's better than all of the disaster movies... Should I be unnerved at how much pleasure you take from watching the world end?"

"I'm sorry if I find the apocalypse soothing." August's tone was cool. "All I'm saying is there's got to be some forensic thingy Rafael can do to figure out what happened."

"The *Magnolia Jane* is at the bottom of the ocean and figuring out what happened won't do anything to help Nora—or Mykal."

Rafael's response got Nora's attention. She fought harder to open her eyes as she asked, "What about Mykal? And where's

Janey?" Her throat hurt and her voice sounded ragged even to her own ears, but it was enough to stop the debate around her. She found herself with August on one side and Rafael on the other, vaguely aware of Leo leaving to find a nurse.

"Thank God you're awake." August crushed Nora in an awkward hug. "You scared me to death, Nora Jones. Don't do that again. Ever."

"What did I do?" Nora's brain hurt from the effort of trying to remember.

"There was an accident, sweetie." August straightened, her eyes meeting Nora's. "The *Magnolia Jane* sank. Mkyal's here in the hospital, too. She got hit on the head pretty hard."

At August's words, the memory flashed through her mind. The loud crack, the flash of white as the boom swung toward her. Nora furrowed her brow, trying to remember more, but there was nothing. "I'd just readjusted the jib sheet. The wind had picked up. I'd turned us around. Did I do this?" Nora looked to Rafael, panic swelling in her chest.

"Hey, listen to me." He spoke for the first time, squeezing her hand tighter and leaning in to get her focus. "You're a good sailor. I've seen you tack the boat. You never miss a step. We don't know what happened yet, but I will find out."

She nodded, reassured by his words.

"All that matters right now is that you're okay. You focus on getting better and leave the mystery solving to me for once," he instructed.

Even in her befuddled state, Nora considered it highly unlikely that would happen. Her expression must have relayed her skepticism because Rafael freed a hand to caress her face.

"I mean it, Nora. Trust me to do my job, just this once. Not because I don't think you can figure it out, but because I'm worried about you. We all are."

"Maybe I'll give you just a few days head start," Nora acquiesced. "My head does hurt."

"You know that's the best you're going to get out of her," August informed him just as they were interrupted by a doctor coming into the room.

August and Rafael stepped back, neither going too far as the doctor checked Nora's eyes and asked her to squeeze his fingers and push against his hand with her feet. She did her best to comply with each instruction, the effort of the concentration wearing her out more than she was willing to admit.

The examination ended with the pronouncement. "You are a very lucky woman."

"I am?" She didn't feel particularly lucky at that moment.

"Other than a couple of cracked ribs and a concussion, I think you're going to walk away from this incident unscathed. It'll take about six weeks for those ribs to heal, so I want you to take it easy while they do. Take off work if you can. I'm prescribing something for pain. Get lots of rest. You might be sore for a few days, and that concussion might make you more sensitive to light. You'll have a bit of brain fog, too. I'd like to keep you overnight for observation since you lost consciousness for so long, but if all goes well, I don't see any reason that we can't send you home in the morning."

Nora started to nod but the movement felt like it was further scrambling her brains, so she stopped. "Thank you, doctor. How's Mykal? The woman who came in with me?"

"We're taking good care of her. I'll let her mother know you're awake and asking about her."

"Thank you," Nora said again, settling back into her pillow. She was worn out from all of the activity and the thinking and, as much as she was concerned for Mykal, what she really wanted and needed at the moment was sleep. Lots and lots of sleep.

"I'm going to let you rest," Rafael announced. "I'll go check on how things are going out at the crash site. Maybe see if there's anything I can run through the mass spectrometer or something."

"Don't tease me right now, Detective Medero. I'm fragile," August informed him.

"You've never been fragile a day in your life, August..." Rafael paused. "What is your last name, anyway?"

"Ray," she answered.

His eyebrows shot up. "August Ray? Kind of makes you sound like you should be a sun-shinier kind of person, doesn't it?"

"Okay, first of all, I am a delight—"

Rafael ducked out of the room before August could get properly wound up, his chuckle lingering in Nora's ears, bringing a smile to her face, which she suspected was his intent all along.

"So, you really don't remember any of it, huh?" August settled into the chair beside Nora's bed.

"I don't—" Nora answered, pausing to see if anything new had shaken loose. "I'd just finished turning the boat around. We were heading back in... and then the sail was swinging toward me."

"Do you remember a super hunky guy hanging around the boat?"

"August, my brain hurts too much to toy with me."

"For real. You and Mykal have a knight in shining armor. Well, shining cargo shorts, anyway. He came by to check on you earlier. Said he pulled you out of the water while his friend called for help. It sounds like you would have drowned if he hadn't come along."

"Really?" Nora crinkled her brow. "I don't remember any-one else being around. No, wait, there was one other boat. The wind was picking up and they'd just headed back, too. Maybe it was them?"

"If that was the only other boat around, then it sounds like it had to be."

"I wonder who it was."

"My guess is that he'll come back by. But he was a cutie. Dark blond hair, pretty blue eyes, and a fantastic body."

Nora raised her eyebrows. "Aren't you engaged?"

"Engaged, not blind."

"Good to know," Leo reminded them of his presence.

August chuckled and waved his concern off. "You know I adore you. I'm just an observant person; that's all."

"Uh-huh." Leo didn't seem sold on her explanation but let it drop—most likely because their little group was joined by Mykal's mom.

"Nora, I'm so glad you're awake," Terra greeted her from the foot of the bed.

"Terra, I'm so sorry. I don't know what happened. Everything seemed fine, and then it just wasn't. How is Mykal?"

"Still unconscious. The MRI showed some swelling on the brain. They're giving her oxygen and some medicine. If it gets worse or doesn't go down soon, they might have to operate to relieve the—to relieve the—" Terra paused a moment to compose herself. "To relieve the pressure."

"I'm so, so sorry." Nora found herself repeating. She wasn't sure what else to say. It seemed unfair that she would be going home in the morning while things looked so dire for Mykal. Nora was beginning to think that she was a jinx to Mykal, and the poor girl would be better off if Nora stopped trying to befriend her.

They talked for a moment more, but Nora was having too hard of a time keeping her eyes open. She fought valiantly, not wanting to be rude, but ultimately the concussion won, and Nora fell asleep mid-conversation. She awoke to find Pru sitting in the chair next to her. She was happy to see her friend but couldn't help wondering when Rafael would be back.

Nora tried to listen as Pru chattered about the gallery but found herself mostly smiling and nodding as the words bounced off of her. Pru paused mid-sentence. Nora's gaze followed her friend's to the doorway, where they'd been joined by a handsome stranger. From the looks of him, Nora guessed he was her knight in shining cargo shorts.

"Hello?" She greeted with a hint of question in her voice.

"Hi." There was a bashfulness about the man that was quite charming. "You don't know me, but I was the one who fished you out of the ocean earlier today. I just wanted to come by to see how you were doing."

"Much better than I was before you pulled me out of the bay," she reassured him. "Thank you for that. It sounds like I would have drowned if you hadn't come along when you did."

"It's lucky I was there."

Nora nodded, not quite sure what else to say. She liked to think that if her brain wasn't injured, she'd be wittier in this moment, but even in her current state she had to admit that probably wasn't true. She was forever thinking of the right thing to say twenty minutes after it was needed.

"I'm Bryan, by the way."

"It's nice to meet you, Bryan. I don't know how to repay you for saving us. Is a lifetime of free books of interest? I own a bookstore."

"Among other things," Pru murmured with a chuckle.

"I don't have that many businesses." Nora tried not to let her exasperation show, earning an outright laugh from Pru.

"I won't keep you," Bryan interjected, his expression a bit perplexed—not that Nora could blame him. "But let me give you my number. Just in case you need anything."

Nora couldn't fathom why she'd need his number but found herself agreeing nonetheless and asking Pru to find her phone and add him as a contact. With that accomplished, he bid them farewell and left the two women alone. They looked at each other in silence for a moment.

"Well, that was certainly odd." Nora pursed her lips.

"All I know is if I nearly drowned, I'd probably get saved by a troll. And you get *that*. Life isn't fair."

"I don't know, getting saved at all when nearly drowning has got to count for something, whatever the rescuer looks like," Nora reasoned.

"Easy for you to say. You're not being rescued by Larry the Cable Guy."

"Who?"

Pru waved a hand dismissively. "Never mind. All I'm saying is you have good taste in saviors."

Nora rested back against her pillow, thinking about Pru's words and the odds that he'd turned his boat around at just the right time to see their accident. It was one of those pivotal moments in life, the kind when stopping to tie your shoes or missing a light can mean the difference between one path and another, between life and death. The universe was weird like that.

Chapter Four

THE SCENERY THAT ROLLED by Nora's window was no different than it had been just a few days before. The rows of green had not changed. The workers were the same. Nora was pretty certain it was even the same head of cabbage lying by the side of the road, no doubt having rolled off a truck on its way to a grocery store somewhere in America. The thought crossed her mind how sad it was; the lonely head of cabbage that would never fulfill its destiny. Some grocer in Minnesota was one head of cabbage short.

"What are you thinking about so hard over there?" Rafael interrupted her mental soliloquy over unrealized purpose.

"Cabbage," she answered honestly with no further explanation.

"I—I don't even know how to respond to that."

Rather than waste precious energy trying to explain, Nora motioned her head toward the window with the seemingly endless fields of cabbage rolling by.

She couldn't say how many miles the awkward silence lingered before Rafael blurted, "I'm glad you're going to stay with August. I know the doctor says you're okay, but I just don't like you being alone these first few nights."

She bit her lip considering, her next words before asking, "Why couldn't you stay with me?"

"Work is just so crazy right now." He seemed a million miles away from her.

"Do you want to talk about it?" She peered over at him, his expression making her think that perhaps he did want to talk about it.

But then his expression changed, and the moment was gone. "I don't want to bore you. Besides, I'd much rather talk about that latest report from Captain Angelou, anyway. Did they really just find a whole other section of the ship?"

Knowing that pressing the matter would be pointless, she obliged him by shifting the conversation. "They did. It was the missing piece of the hull. Gregory says it will extend the recovery operation by at least six months, but it's worth it. Some of the artifacts they're bringing up are unprecedented. Poor Ivy, though."

"Why's that?"

"I think she and Gregory would be dating by now if they didn't work together. I fully expect one of them to ask the other out when Gregory buys out my shares of the salvage business."

"If that's the case, then maybe you should sell him the shares a little earlier than planned."

"Maybe." Nora's tone was noncommittal. Rafael wasn't wrong, and Nora had said repeatedly she wanted out of the salvage business, but when it came to it, she was finding herself loathe to sign over something that had been so integral to who her uncle Walter had been. Even more so having lost the *Magnolia Jane*.

When Nora's phone rang, she was almost relieved because it saved her from having to explore all the feelings the previous conversation had surfaced. That is, she was relieved until she saw the caller ID.

Rafael glanced over at her sigh. "I can't say I'm sorry to be off Emily duty."

She couldn't blame him. He'd been a champ, relaying information to Nora's mother up to this point—and managing to keep the older Jones woman from hopping on the next flight to Florida. She supposed it was her turn to tag in.

"Hey, Mom," Nora answered the phone. "How are you?"

"How am I? How are you? I'm worried about my daughter, that's how am I."

"You don't need to worry. I'm okay, promise."

"How can you be okay? You nearly died."

"Nearly being the operative word," Nora interrupted before course-correcting. "And I didn't nearly die. The doctor assures me I'm quite well."

"Maybe I should talk to Rafael. I don't think you're telling me the truth."

"Raf is busy right now, but I'm telling the truth. I'm okay."

"Sofía and I are supposed to leave on our murder cruise tomorrow, but we can cancel if you're not well."

"Murder cruise?" Nora asked. "Do I want to know what that is?"

"Like a murder mystery dinner, but a cruise."

"Huh. Sounds interesting."

"It does, but we'll cancel if you need us to come home."

"I wouldn't dream of it," Nora said, not bothering to remind her mother that she lived in California, so Florida wasn't exactly home. Nora was a little afraid the reminder would prompt her mother to buy a place in St. Augustine. "Go on your cruise and tell me all about it when you get back."

Rafael waited for Nora to hang up the phone before saying, "I suspect she wanted you to ask her to cancel."

"Maybe." Nora almost felt guilty. "But there isn't really anything she can do. And I need quiet more than anything right now."

"So, uh, am I the only one concerned by the friendship your mother and my grandmother have struck up?"

"Oh, no, it's terrifying," Nora quickly reassured him.

Pulling down the driveway of Quirkiosities did not have the same effect on her as it had on her last visit. She was sore and tired, and her brain hurt. And there was this ugly feeling that looked a lot like guilt lying under the surface, tainting pretty much everything at the moment. But Margo was suffering from none of those things, so she shifted in her seat, whining with excitement as she recognized how close they were to one of the few places where she could truly soar off-lead.

Their car was met by a little welcome party. August, Leo, Pru, and even Ivy had shown up. Raymond was there as well, at the back of the crowd looking incredibly uncomfortable and perhaps a bit concerned for his white linen suit as one of the farm dogs brushed past.

Nora was at once moved by how sweet it was of everyone to drive all that way and exhausted from the effort of the ride there. Her friends most likely sensed as much because after a short visit, Nora found herself tucked in bed in one of the guest cabins with Margo lying at her feet, the dog's warm body a reassuring presence that however topsy-turvy her world might feel at the moment, all would be well.

Despite the awkwardness in the car, Nora was sad to see Raf leave so quickly. She had hoped, on some level, that he would stay and keep her company. Her head still hurt too badly to read, so she found herself doing something she rarely did: She watched TV, or rather let it flow around her while she dozed in and out of sleep. The next two days passed roughly the same, in a haze of sleep and television and thought interspersed by visits from August or Pru. Very noticeable was the absence of Rafael, though she was surprised when her knight in shining armor showed up. She supposed she should start calling him Bryan at some point.

Nora wanted to ask how he'd found her but that felt rude, so she let it go, assuming that August had told him, and simply enjoyed the visit from someone who wasn't hovering over her like she might expire at any moment—or walling her out, or whatever it was Rafael was doing these days. She found that Bryan was easy to talk to, or rather listen to. Perhaps he knew she didn't really have it in her to make much conversation, and so he chatted easily, filling her in with stories of his days in the military.

It was during that conversation that Nora learned there was apparently still a law somewhere in Kansas that made it illegal to park your camel on the street. She knew this because at one point in time, Bryan had been arrested for parking his camel in the wrong spot—they were supposed to be parked in the alley, not on the main road.

"I need to know the story behind this," Nora insisted.

"Eh." He shrugged. "The circus was in town. I might have had one too many when someone bet me that I wouldn't ride a camel."

"So, did you steal the camel or rent it? I don't understand how they let you just leave with their camel."

"I can be persuasive."

"While I don't doubt that, I find it hard to believe anyone can be *that* persuasive."

He flashed her a grin that made her blush right down to her toes.

"What happened after you persuaded the circus to loan you a camel?"

"I rode it back to the bar, parked it out front, and went in to claim my free beer."

"You did all of that for a beer?"

He nodded. "Sadly, I didn't even get my prize. The sheriff followed me in and asked whose camel was parked out front. I said, 'mine,' and promptly found myself in jail for violating an ordinance that was still on the books from horse and buggy days."

"Who knew?" Nora asked, amused.

"As it turns out, commanding officers get irritated when they have to come and bail you out of jail for parking a camel on the street illegally."

"I'll file that away for future reference," she promised dutifully. Hours after he'd left, she was still chuckling about the story. She tried to recount the adventure to August, but she must have failed in capturing the humor of it because August merely arched an eyebrow and replied with, "Uh-huh."

She was surprised when Raymond stopped by unannounced the next day, claiming he missed his two favorite girls.

"I'd say how sweet, but I know you mean Nora and Margo," August teased. "I'll leave you two to visit; apparently there's a goat stuck in a tree or something." With that, she left them alone on the front porch swing.

"You know," Raymond mused. "That's not a sentence you hear every day."

"I find that happens quite a bit in August's presence." Nora wished for a moment she could go watch August try to get said goat out of the aforementioned tree before turning her attention to her guest. "Two visits to the country in one week, Raymond. Are you worried about me or is this a new, adventuresome chapter in your life, full of a flagrant disregard for your linen suits?"

"Always one to cut right to the chase, Nora, my dear. It's one of the many things I love about you." Raymond patted her hand in an affectionate gesture before clearing his throat and forging ahead. "I just thought it might be good to remind you that I'm still on retainer, should you need me."

Nora shifted so she could see him better, trying to read his face as she asked, "Will I be needing a lawyer for anything in particular?"

"I hope not, but there's still a lot up in the air with the accident."

"Do you think Terra will sue me?"

"My intent was not to make you worry about things that have not and might never happen. Only to remind you that I'm here, should things get unpleasant."

Nora slowly nodded, taking in his words and turning over the unpleasant possibilities in her mind. She shoved the dark thoughts aside and smiled at him. "Thank you, my friend. Now, how about we go see if we can find some lemonade or something? I'm thirsty."

"We could—" he paused briefly. "Or we could go watch August try to get a goat out of a tree."

"I like that idea," Nora quickly agreed.

Unfortunately, August had already rescued the wayward animal by the time they found her. All the walking was enough to completely deplete Nora's energy, so she returned to her bed while Raymond retreated to a world safe for linen suits.

By the fourth day of her convalescence, Nora was climbing the walls. She knew she wasn't supposed to drive yet, so she begged August to take her and Margo home. She wanted, no, needed to be in her own space.

While on their way back to town, Nora got a text from Terra that Mykal had awakened without needing surgery, but she was still hospitalized. So, Nora sweet-talked August into taking her to the hospital for a quick visit after dropping Margo off at the house.

She was relieved to find Mykal sitting up in bed, looking almost like herself. When the woman greeted them with a smile, Nora wanted to weep with relief, throw herself at the foot of the girl's bed, and beg forgiveness. Instead, she smiled nervously and said, "Hey."

Not her most eloquent utterance ever, but given the circumstances, not the worst she could have done, either. When Nora started to run through the apology that she had rehearsed in her mind 1,000 times, Mykal interrupted her.

"Nora, it wasn't your fault."

"How can you say that? I was the one who took you out sailing. I was the one who was in charge of the boat. I was the one who untied the rigging to readjust things—I don't see how this wasn't my fault." Nora felt like she was in danger of drowning in the whirlpool of emotions that her words whipped up.

Mykal looked at her quietly for a second before asking, "What did you do wrong, then? Tell me."

Nora thought about it, and she honestly couldn't answer, for all of the time she'd spent thinking about it over the last few days. It plagued her that she still didn't know what she had done wrong, what she could have done differently.

Mykal gave a short, decisive nod. "Exactly. You can't tell me what you did wrong because you didn't do anything wrong. I don't know how the accident happened. All I know is that you told me to get out of the way of the boom, so I did. You turned the boat around and things were fine. I'd just shifted positions to watch some dolphins when something hit me, and I don't think it was your fault."

As much as Nora wanted to believe her, she also suspected that Mykal was just about the sweetest person on the planet and was letting her off the hook when she didn't deserve it.

"Well, thank you, Mykal," Nora acquiesced. She wasn't going to argue with the person who had just sustained a head injury on her boat. But even if she held her tongue, Nora wasn't convinced she should let go of her guilt just yet.

"Oh, look, you got flowers." August changed the conversation. "They're so pretty! Do you have an admirer we don't know about Mykal?"

The young woman flushed, barely glancing over at the flowers before looking back to her friends and then looking down again, almost as if she didn't know where her eyes should land.

"Okay, now I really want to know who they're from," August said.

"Sorry; there wasn't a note." Mykal didn't seem particularly sorry. And despite the lack of note, Nora had the distinct impression she knew exactly who they were from but didn't want to say.

Given her cagey demeanor over the flowers, Nora wondered if they were from the ex-boyfriend Mykal had mentioned on the boat.

Rather than allowing August to pursue it, Nora said, "Well, they're lovely," and then sat tentatively on the edge of Mykal's bed and changed the conversation. "Have you met our rescuer yet?"

Mykal's brow furrowed in confusion, making Nora think she'd yet to hear of him, let alone meet him. It struck Nora as odd, that he'd shown up all the way out at the farm to see her and had not checked in yet on Mykal, who was obviously the more injured of the two.

Regardless, she smiled and said, "He's really sweet. His name is Bryan. He was in the boat that turned around right about the time we did. When he saw we were in trouble, he and his friends helped us out. I guess if Bryan hadn't pulled me out of the water, I would have drowned."

"Sounds like he's your guardian angel, Nora."

"Why can't I have a guardian angel like that?" August muttered under her breath.

Nora stopped and looked at her friend, resisting the urge to roll her eyes. "Again, August, you are engaged."

"And I love my fiancé very much," August reassured her. "I'm just saying you got a cute guardian angel."

"Really? I think I want to hear about this," Mykal perked up, making Nora wonder what it was about gossiping about boys that women never seem to grow out of. It seemed to bring out the teenage girl in most women, regardless of circumstance.

Their conversation didn't get too far before it was interrupted by Rhett Davis, the young police officer who had become Nora's friend when he'd been assigned to her police protection detail once upon a time.

"Rhett!" Nora's smile was genuine. He truly was one of her favorite people.

"Nora, I'm so glad you're doing okay," Rhett greeted her. "I've been worried about you."

"I'm okay. Takes more than a swim in the ocean to get me down. I'm still a little sore, but they say the ribs should heal soon. And the brain, too. Gosh, I hope the brain heals soon."

"Nora, sweetie, you're babbling again." August patted her arm gently.

"Right." Nora grimaced. The rambling seemed to be a side effect of the concussion. "What's up, Rhett? Or did you just pop by to listen to me ramble, despite August's assertion otherwise?"

Officer Davis shifted from one foot to the other. "I just came by to see if you remember anything else. I mean, I know you gave your statement once already, but you'd been so foggy on the details. And I know with brain injuries, you know, sometimes things come back to you after a little while. So, do you remember anything else about that day? Anything seem odd or out of place?"

Nora tried to reach back into her memory, pleased to see it didn't cause the physical pain it did a couple of days ago. Unfortunately, it didn't turn up anything else.

"I really can't remember anything new; I'm sorry. Mykal, can you think of anything?"

She shook her head. "I don't know enough about sailboats to tell you what's normal and what's not. But I don't remember anybody being weird that day. It was a pretty day and we were having fun. Everything seemed to be going well until it wasn't."

"Okay." He nodded, taking in their words. "It's really important that you tell me if you do remember anything, Nora."

"What's this about, Rhett?" Warning bells sounded in Nora's mind. "I mean, I'm devastated over losing *Janey*, but accidents do happen."

"Nora, this wasn't an accident. The *Magnolia Jane* was sabotaged."

Chapter Five

"WHAT?" CAME THE CHORUS from all three women.

"Detective Medero didn't tell you?"

"No, I haven't seen Detective Medero in a couple of days." Nora wasn't sure she succeeded at keeping the irritation out of her voice, but the look on August's face said she caught the fact that Nora didn't use Raf's first name.

"Oh, well, then maybe I shouldn't have said anything." Rhett frowned and then a look of panic flitted across his face. "Please don't tell him I said anything."

"He won't hear it from me." Even as she said it, she wasn't sure how she'd keep that promise. Everything in her wanted to march straight over to Rafael's and read him the riot act for keeping this from her, but the instant she did, he'd know where she'd heard it.

Nora managed to keep her face impassive for the rest of the visit. If Rhett or Mykal noticed anything amiss, neither commented on it. August, however, was not about to let Nora get off that easily. At least she had the kindness to wait until they were in the van alone to bring it up, though.

"So, Detective Medero, huh?" August focused on the left turn she was making as she said the words.

Nora looked out the window, feeling a bit like a petulant teenager when she didn't bother to answer.

"I'm sure he has what he thinks is a good reason," August continued. "I mean, don't get me wrong—I'd be furious at him, too—but I suspect he thinks he's doing the right thing."

Nora closed her eyes for a moment, frustrated at the tears that wanted to surface. "I think we should talk about something else." She opened her eyes and glanced over at August. "How is the wedding planning going?"

August winced.

"That bad?"

"As soon as you say the word 'wedding,' the price of everything quadruples. At least."

"Surely not."

"It's a total racket. I'm about ready to start telling venues I'm calling about my son's bar mitzvah."

"Why not just say a party?"

August shrugged lightly. "Bar mitzvah sounds more fun."

"And when you show up in a white dress?" Nora wondered.

"What are they going to do? Kick me out? Hurriedly tack on a bunch of fees and demand a wedding planner be on premises at once?"

"Surely it's not that bad?" Nora hoped August was exaggerating.

"I'm serious. Do you know venues require you to have a wedding planner? And if you don't, they tack on a $500 fee and make you use theirs for the day."

"If an affordable venue is the holdup—" Nora began, only to be cut off by August.

"If you offer to pay for the wedding, I swear I will replace you as maid of honor."

Nora closed her mouth and frowned at August. "That feels uncalled for."

"I adore you," August said. "And I appreciate everything you've done for me, for Charlotte, and for Leo. But no more. It's just too much. Your money is not why we're friends."

"I know that." Nora fell quiet for a moment. While she did know it, she realized it was quite nice to hear August say the words. And even though she'd absolutely been about to offer to pay for the wedding, she wasn't about to admit that now. "I was just going to suggest that you use Quirkiosities for the venue. If it goes well, maybe we'll open it up for other weddings. That could be a good revenue stream."

August pursed her lips for a moment. "That's not a bad idea."

"Thank you."

"And Ivy will be so proud of you for adding revenue streams without adding another business."

"I thought so." Nora sighed and rested her head back against the seat, closing her eyes again. All of the conversation and sunshine were making her concussed brain hurt. Besides, she still had to figure out what she was going to do with the knowledge that her beloved *Magnolia Jane* had been sabotaged—and what she was going to say to Rafael when she saw him.

She tried to honor her promise to Rhett. For all of three hours after August dropped her off, she tossed and turned, trying to take a nap. When that clearly wasn't going to happen, she went downstairs to turn on a record, hoping the music would help clear her mind. She closed the curtains, dimmed the lights, and tried to mellow out.

When that didn't work, she called to check in on the shop. Reginald assured her all was quiet and told her not to worry about coming in to close up, that he'd take care of it. While she appreciated the help, not having anything to do wasn't helping get her mind off of things.

She tried making a mental list of who might want to hurt her. Of course, the grudge could have been against Lucca or even Walter. Maybe the saboteur didn't know the *Magnolia Jane* had passed hands. She'd never been in this particular situation before, but it seemed odd to her that nobody from the police had contacted her about the discovery. Besides Rhett, but he didn't count.

By that evening, she'd run herself in enough mental circles to have given up all hope of calming down. If rest was going to elude her, that left her with only one reasonable course of action: she called an Uber to drive her over to Rafael's apartment.

Having been raised by a mother who was offended by something as obscene as visible emotion, Nora generally tried to regulate what she allowed others to see, especially when it came to something as base as anger. This, however, was not one of those times.

The more she thought about it, the angrier she got at Rafael. Despite knowing how racked with guilt she was, he'd made the conscious decision not to share this crucial piece of information with her. It felt like a betrayal on so many levels. Emily Jones would have been horrified by the swirling wrath that was nearly palpable around Nora by the time she knocked on his door. She didn't even let him get a hello out before starting her rant.

"How dare you? How dare you keep this from me? I would have expected this from some mouth-breathing Neanderthal, but not you."

"Excuse me?" Rafael blinked in the face of her fury.

"Don't pretend that you don't know what I'm talking about." She folded her arms across her chest and narrowed her eyes at him.

Clearly taken aback by her vehemence, Rafael reached out, not to touch her but to motion downward, as if he were trying to calm a wild animal. "Nora, there's a lot going on here that you don't understand. I just needed to get to the bottom of some things before I said anything."

"We are not that couple. You don't get to decide for me what my little brain can or cannot handle."

"It wasn't like that." He shook his head. "I was trying to sort out what was even going on. I didn't want to give you half-truths—and I'm going to wring Rhett's neck for saying something to you. He should never have let that go outside the precinct."

"If you so much as give that man the side-eye Rafael Santos Medero, I will be livid with you."

"Isn't that what you are now?"

"I will be livider with you," she amended.

"Is that a word?"

"Are we really going to argue about this right now, too?" Nora asked

He cocked his head. "I don't know. Is it more livid?

"I'm pretty sure it's livider. How about we just say furious? Are you comfortable with that word?"

"Grammatically? Yes. But I'm not sure I want the reality of it." There was resignation in Rafael's voice.

"Then be nice to Rhett. You know I was going to find out about this sooner rather than later anyway. I mean, if it's sabotage, won't there be a detective assigned to the case?"

"It's with Fish & Wildlife now, but I imagine the sheriff will be part of the investigation, too."

"But not you?"

"Uh, no. Not me."

"Is that a jurisdiction thing? I mean, is that normal for the municipal police to not have anything to do with the investigation?"

"There's a lot happening at the moment that's completely out of my control."

"Do you want to talk about it?" She reached out for his hand, her entire demeanor shifting in response to the look on his face. She saw pain there.

Raf shoved his hands in his pockets and took a step back. "I'm sorry, Nora, I really can't talk about it."

She stared at him for a moment, sadness stirring where anger had been just moments before. "Okay then."

Not sure what was even left to say, Nora regarded him, trying to decide if this was one of those stay-and-fight moments or a give-them-space kind of thing. Given the throbbing in her head, she didn't trust herself not to say something she couldn't take back. So, she kissed his cheek and left, her heart breaking because it felt like something between them had shifted.

Even though everyone kept assuring Nora they had everything under control, and she should rest, being so out of step with the rest of the world made her feel like she was constantly forgetting something mission-critical, and it was all going to spiral out of control while she whiled away the days on her couch watching BBC whodunits.

Nora had been so upset with Rafael that when she'd found out a different investigator had been assigned to the case, she was kind of happy. Maybe this new investigator would respect that she had a stake in this, too. After all, it was her boat, and it had been her life put at risk. But as the days wore on without a word from Sherriff Reynolds, Nora began to wonder if anybody was going to investigate anything at all. Maybe what happened to her beloved *Magnolia Jane* didn't matter to anyone besides her.

August, on the other hand, wasn't so quick to write it off. When she stopped by Nora's with a pile of bridal magazines and announced that they'd set a date, so planning needed to begin in earnest, Nora had filled her friend in on the radio silence concerning the investigation as they sat in her living room floor, pouring over the magazines for inspiration.

"Are you sure that they're just ignoring you?"

"What do you mean?" Nora asked, pointing to the dress on the left when August held two up for Nora's opinion.

August glanced at the dress again before nodding approvingly and marking the page with a Post-it. "Could there be something else going on here?"

"What else could it be?" Nora struggled to wrap her brain around what could possibly keep them from investigating.

"I don't know." August held up two more dresses for Nora's input, this time wrinkling her nose at Nora's choice and setting both pictures aside. "It just seems awfully strange to me. I mean, I guess I could understand it if you were a nobody, but you have money. People tend to pay attention when bad things happen to people with money. It just seems a little odd to me that no one is paying attention to this."

Some part of Nora wanted to write August's words off as cynicism, but she had to acknowledge her lived experience was different from August's. They'd walked very different paths, and Nora couldn't question whether or not her friend's experience was valid just because it had not been her own.

By the time the stack of bridal magazines was sufficiently covered in sticky notes, August had filled her wedding notebook with ideas and checklists and Nora was exhausted.

"I saw that," August told her when Nora failed to stifle a yawn. "Why don't you go take a nap while I get dinner started?"

"Don't you need to get back to Charlotte?"

"She and Leo are having a date tonight. We're having a girls' night."

"A girls' night?" Nora wasn't sure she was up for that.

"Don't worry, a low-key girls' night. Ivy is coming over. We'll hang out here, but we figured your convalescence was driving you crazy."

"What gave it away?" Nora thought she'd done a fine job of keeping her restlessness tamped down.

August raised her eyebrows before picking her phone up off the table and opening it and holding it out for Nora to see. It took a second, but she recognized their chat.

"Sorry." Nora squeaked, a bit embarrassed to realize just how much she'd been texting her friends. It hadn't seemed like quite so much at the time, but scrolling through it now, she supposed she had gotten a bit talkative in her boredom.

"I don't mind a bit," August promised. "But I thought you could maybe use something besides the phone to interact with."

"It's possible," Nora conceded. "But I will take you up on that nap first."

Her intent was to rest her eyes a moment; she didn't think she'd actually be able to fall asleep. But she was so disoriented when Margo chuffed a while later, it was clear she'd passed out the second her head hit the pillow. Nora couldn't say how long she'd been out, but it was dark out, and judging from Margo's pacing, they had company.

She gave herself a minute to get oriented before padding to the bathroom to splash some water on her face and run a brush through her hair. Nora eyed herself skeptically in the mirror. It wasn't great, but it was the best she could do under the circumstances.

By the time she made it downstairs, Ivy was perched on a barstool at her kitchen island, sipping a glass of pinot grigio and chatting with August, who was putting the finishing touches on what looked to be lemon garlic linguine with shrimp on the side and a giant salad to go with it.

"You are too good to me." Nora took a deep breath and sighed happily. "Dinner looks and smells amazing."

"There she is," Ivy greeted her with a smile. "You're looking better each day, girl."

"You're too good to me as well." Nora hugged Ivy before looking back at August. "Is there anything I can do to help?"

"Nope." August shook her head cheerfully. "I'm just about to pull the bread out of the oven and then we're all ready."

Not needed, Nora went to fill Margo's dish so the dog would stop pestering Ivy for attention before taking her seat at the table.

Dinner tasted even better than it smelled. Conversation flowed freely and even if Nora couldn't keep up quite as well as usual and talked a bit softer, she realized August had been exactly right—she'd desperately needed this.

"Is there an update on Mykal?" Ivy asked.

Nora brightened. "There is. She's getting out tomorrow."

"That's certainly cause for celebration." Ivy lifted her glass in acknowledgment.

"I'm so relieved," Nora agreed. "I've been worried about her."

"Any news on the Mag—" Ivy must have noticed August shaking her head and frowning because she paused, her face faltering before continuing. "—mangos?"

"The mangos?" Nora's eyebrows shot up. "No. I don't think I've heard any news about mangos. But the *Magnolia Jane* is a total loss."

"Sorry." Ivy chuckled ruefully. "It was the best I could come up with when I saw August's abort mission face."

"It was a valiant effort, on both your parts," Nora commended. "I've been on the phone with the insurance company half the day dealing with it. They won't pay out until the investigation is complete, but I can't seem to get anyone at the sheriff's office—or fish and wildlife—to give me an update on it, so round and round I go."

"Well, Gregory should be back tomorrow," Ivy said. "From the tone of his voice last time we spoke, I think he has good news for you, at least. He wanted to tell us both in person, but he sounded like a kid who'd just gotten an Xbox for Christmas, so they must have found something good in that new ship section."

"It'll be nice to see him." Nora meant it. She genuinely liked and respected the captain of her salvage boat. "How long is he back for?"

"A week?" Ivy's tone suggested that was a guess.

"The two of you should stop waiting for him to buy the business and just go out already," August interjected.

Ivy stabbed her salad with more force than was necessary. "Talk to Gregory about that one."

"Does that mean I have permission to?" August waggled her eyebrows and laughed. "Because you know I will."

Ivy cracked a grin. "Let me think about that."

Their banter made her mind turn back to Rafael. He hadn't called or texted since their last encounter. Neither had she, but she felt like the ball was in his court at this point.

"Have you ever wondered what goes through their minds?" Nora mused aloud. "I mean, what makes them think 'I'm going to lie to her about this? Yeah, that'll work well for me.'"

August chuckled and gave a little shrug and said, "I try not to think too hard about what goes through their minds."

"Does anything go through their minds? Are we giving them too much credit?" Ivy asked.

"I'm not going to point out that you sounded a touch bitter there," August said lightly.

Ivy shrugged and took a sip of her wine.

"I just really gave Raf more credit than that." Nora scowled at the linguini that refused to stay on her fork.

"That's the thing about putting people on pedestals," August said gently. "They're human, so they inevitably fall."

Chapter Six

August's words were still bumping around Nora's brain the next morning as she watched her coffee bloom before pressing it. Mykal had taught her the trick to a good French press was to pour in just enough water to cover the grounds, wait forty-five seconds for the coffee grounds to release their carbon dioxide so the water could unlock the flavor, and then finish pouring the water in.

"Why does this feel like the longest forty-five seconds in the world?" Nora asked. Margo barely flicked her ears in response. Nora smiled at the dog and went back to watching the mahogany coffee grounds swirl and blossom, wondering if Pru ever associated visual stimulation with a particular sound or if it was only ever the other way around. And if she did, what would she think coffee sounded like?

Her doorbell rang, startling her. She glanced at the clock; it was only a few minutes after seven, still too early for a casual visit. Nora quickly poured the rest of the water over the coffee grounds and went to answer the door, hoping that she wouldn't regret answering it in lounge pants and a messy bun.

She wasn't sure whom she was expecting to see standing on the other side of that door, but it certainly wasn't a bowling shirt clad mobster—or rather, retired mobster.

"You don't even have a hello for an old friend?" he asked after a full thirty seconds of her staring at him speechless in her doorway.

With that, she shook off her stupor and threw her arms around his neck in a hug that surprised them both.

"What on earth are you doing here, Lucca? Get in here before anybody sees you!" She dragged him into the house and closed the door behind him.

Having still not gotten over her fear of Lucca, Margo made herself scarce as soon as she realized who their guest was. Nora mentally checked guard dog off the list of possible occupations for her four-legged friend.

"Why are you here?" Nora asked again. "Won't this get you kicked out of witness protection?"

"Somebody can't go after my daughter and my friend and not expect a response."

"Do you think maybe that's what they were going for?" Nora wondered aloud. "Could it be possible someone did this to flush you out of hiding?"

"It is a possibility," he conceded. "But the fact remains that this cannot go answered."

"Assuming it was about you," Nora pointed out. "It's also entirely possible that this had nothing to do with you, and you just put yourself in danger for no reason."

The look he gave her suggested that he thought it was always about him, and she was crazy to think it could be otherwise.

"Have you been staying out of trouble?" The fatherly tone in his voice amused her.

The corner of her lip twitched. "Absolutely. Other than the near-death experience, that is."

"You know what I'm asking you." His amusement did not match her own.

"I haven't had anything to do with the mob. Haven't even met the new guy. Don't even know his name."

Lucca lowered his brows as if he wasn't sure he believed her. "Well, he knows you."

"Don't look angry at me," she admonished. "How is that my fault?"

If he had more to say on the topic, he opted to let it drop. "What about your mother? Has she been in town recently?"

Nora shook her head. "Nope. She's on a murder mystery cruise with Rafael's abuela."

"There's a terrifying thought," Lucca muttered.

"That's what Raf and I said."

"Nora, I hate to ask this of you," Lucca hesitated. "But please don't tell your boyfriend I'm here."

"That shouldn't be too difficult," she responded ruefully. "He's not talking to me much these days."

Lucca frowned. "I'm sorry to hear that. I expected better of that young man."

"What's up with you two, anyway?" she asked, curious about the backstory she could sense but neither had been forthcoming about.

"I'm not sure it's my story to tell."

Nora didn't try to hide her displeasure at that response. "I'm getting really tired of you boys being so cryptic."

Lucca chuckled "Maybe we know how much you love a good mystery."

"Yes, I'm sure that's it." Nora didn't believe for a second that it was. "As much as I would love to stay and visit, I feel like the longer you're in this house, the more likely you are to be discovered."

"Well, I'm not leaving until we know what happened, and I know that you're safe. I'll check into a hotel if you're worried about getting me getting you in trouble," he said.

"You will do no such thing!" She cut him off. "If I can't talk you into going home, then I know just the place to stash you until we get this figured out."

Nora supposed she should run her plan by August, but she knew her friend well enough to know she wouldn't care—it was Leo who would need convincing. He was protective of his new little family. So much so, that his producer was having a hard time getting him back out in the field for filming. She did, however, take a moment to text that she would be bringing someone by in a bit. Partly out of politeness, partly because she didn't know what August and Leo did in their free time when Charlotte was at school, and Nora had no desire to walk in on anything she wouldn't be able to unsee.

It didn't take her long to get ready, though the process was made slightly longer by constantly tripping over Margo, who stayed glued to Nora's side, eyeing Lucca warily like he was going to abscond with her at any moment. Despite that, she soon had the dog and mobster loaded into her car and the trio was heading west, away from the beaches of Anastasia Island. As the dense tourist attractions gave way to miles of green in either direction, Lucca glanced over at her warily. "You're not going to drop me alongside the road like an old dog, are you?"

"You are an old dog, but I have no intention of dumping you beside the road," she assured him.

"You wound me with your words, my dear."

"It's the concussion."

"Should you be driving?" he asked.

"Possibly not," she admitted, amending her answer when she glanced over and saw the concern clearly etched on his face. "I mean, absolutely. I'm fine."

"You're a terrible liar."

Nora shrugged lightly, not even trying to deny it. "You're not wrong."

An awkward silence descended. Lucca coughed uncomfortably. Seeking to fill the gap, Nora turned on the radio and was rewarded with the distinctive vocals of one of her favorite bands. Despite the ever-present headache, she turned it up a notch and sang along softly to the Cranberries' *Linger*.

Before long, Lucca's gravelly voice was lamenting being a fool, too. Surprised, Nora glanced over at him, her gaze darting back to the road in hopes her gawking wouldn't silence him. This was a new side to Lucca, and she enjoyed it very much.

"What?"

Nora inwardly grimaced at being caught. "Nothing. I guess I'm just surprised you know this song."

"I can't appreciate good music?'

She opened her mouth to protest but then noticed his expression. "You're messing with me."

"I am."

"You've got all kinds of delightful layers, don't you?"

"Something like that." The corner of his mouth ticked up despite his deadpan delivery.

Smiling, Nora went back to singing, her grin deepening as Lucca's voice grew stronger. One song melted into the next and they were soon pulling down the gravel drive of Quirkiosities.

Buck showed up to usher them in, earning Nora another rueful look from Lucca "You're certain you're not just dumping me like a stray?"

"That's the welcoming crew," Nora explained. "Just stay out of the liger and the gator enclosures, and you'll be fine. Besides, you're not the first witness we've sheltered here. Ferdinand seems very happy in his new home."

"Ferdinand?" Lucca raised his eyebrows inquisitively.

"The alligator. He was and unwilling participant in an art gallery heist," Nora said, as if were a perfectly rational explanation.

Whether the explanation made sense to him or not, any trepidation Lucca still held melted away when he saw August coming to greet them. Nora supposed she could have just told him where she was taking him—he'd always liked August—but it had been more fun watching him squirm. She wondered briefly if her brain injury really had made her meaner. Or maybe it was just spending too much time with August. The wild-haired hippie did have an ornery streak.

Ornery or not, August barely missed a beat, even as she registered who Nora had brought to her door. She greeted Lucca with a warm hug and insisted he come inside for a glass of sweet tea. After ensuring they were alone in the house, Nora filled August in on the current predicament, ending with the big ask, "... and I was hoping he might be able to stay here with you, just until we get this all figured out."

August didn't hesitate. "Absolutely."

"I'm sorry to spring this on you, but I didn't think it was something I should ask over the phone."

"Probably not. And I don't mind, anyway."

"And you're sure this won't cause you any trouble?" Lucca asked.

August gave a carefree shrug and a warm smile. "Nonsense—who's gonna know? We're not open yet, so it's just us out here. And if anybody does show up and ask, we'll just tell them you're the snake wrangler or something."

"Snake wrangler?" Lucca paled.

"I wouldn't expect you to actually wrangle snakes," she assured him. "It just gives you an excuse for being here."

"What other animals do you have?" he asked.

Nora's lips twitched; she was positive he was hoping that would come off as much more nonchalant than it had. "Lucca Buccio... are you afraid of snakes?"

"Afraid is a strong word," he corrected. "I just have a healthy respect for them."

"Huh." Nora let out a short laugh. "You learn something new every day."

Chapter Seven

"ARE YOU SURE WE should be doing this right now?" Nora asked. "I mean, is it really the best time to have a bunch of strangers out to Quirkiosities?"

August glanced up from the tofu she was browning. "Do we have much choice? Wouldn't it raise more suspicion if we canceled after Pru put so much work into organizing everything? Besides, nobody's going to recognize Lucca in his current state."

Nora chuckled softly to herself. She had to admit August was right about that. Lucca currently looked more like a Crocodile Hunter fanboy than a mob boss, having finally embraced his new title of snake wrangler. Not that he'd step foot anywhere near the reptile cabin, but he looked the part.

First to arrive was Pru, bumping down the drive in a beat-up old Toyota pickup with a man in her passenger seat that had to be Ivy's brother. Nora could tell even at a distance that he was every bit as beautiful as his sister, with the same well-defined cheekbones and jawline, only broader and more masculine. He was tall and trim but well-muscled enough that neither Nora nor August could help murmuring appreciation when he unfurled from Pru's tiny truck.

"I'm curious to meet Ivy's parents. They must be stunning," August observed as the tall black man and petite blonde ambled toward them, chatting easily with one another.

Nora couldn't help it; she was playing matchmaker in her mind.

"Hey, guys!" Pru greeted them each with a hug. Nora tried not to wince but must have failed because Pru whispered a guilty "sorry" before continuing with introductions. "Marcus, this is August, and the fragile one is Nora. Guys, this is Ivy's little brother, Marcus."

"Little?" August arched an eyebrow, causing him to chuckle with a hint of embarrassment.

"It's nice to meet you, Marcus," Nora extended a hand. "And I'm not fragile, just on the mend."

"It's nice to meet you, too." His hand was warm and strong. "Ivy told me about your boating accident. That's terrible."

"Thank you," Nora replied. "Are you enjoying St. Augustine so far?"

"I am, thanks. Just getting settled in. The studio is amazing, and Pru has been so helpful."

"That's wonderful." Nora couldn't help sneaking a hopeful glance at Pru, who returned the look with one that clearly said, *don't go there.*

The rest of the crew trickled in. Pru had certainly pulled together the eclectic bunch. But then, Nora suspected any group of artists would be an eclectic bunch. The energy on the farm changed with their arrival. There was a buzz in the air that felt more like a party brewing than a workday, a feeling helped along by August setting out a veritable feast of a buffet. Nora wasn't vegan, but she did appreciate August's ability to make vegetables appetizing and found herself grazing way more than she'd intended to throughout the day.

Despite the festive atmosphere, everybody set to work soon after the hellos were said, each claiming a space on the walls around Ferdinand's new enclosure to paint their piece of the mural. Nora protested when she was handed a brush, not wanting to destroy their art, but August was rather tenacious when she wanted to be. So, she dutifully painted daisies in her corner because it was the one thing that she knew how to doodle.

Nora was deep in concentration, debating whether or not she was gutsy enough to try shadowing on her daisies when Lucca came to lean against the wall. He watched her for a moment before speaking in a low voice. "I know this isn't what you want to hear, but I still think you're caught up in a family dispute."

She'd had entirely too much interaction with the mafia for a bookshop owner, by her way of thinking. "Why would they come after me? I own a bookstore."

"You do way more than own a bookstore, Nora, and we both know it. We also both know that you're responsible for considerable disruptions to the family business since your appearance in St. Augustine."

"But I don't mean to disrupt business," she protested. "It just sort of happens. And that last time was my mother's fault, not mine."

Lucca chuckled softly. "Yes, I heard about that. Listen, all I'm saying is let me go into town. Ask a few questions. I still have people who are loyal to me."

"And you also still have a target on you. If you show your face, we won't have to worry about getting you back into witness protection because you'll be dead."

"Ever the optimist." His tone was light, but he let the subject drop. His brow furrowed as he studied her artwork. "Those flowers need a shadow. They look like they're floating."

Nora opened her mouth to defend herself, but he was gone, leaving her to continue her mental debate as to whether or not she was brave enough to try shadowing. It occurred to her that there was a certain measure of humor in the fact that she could spend millions of dollars purchasing a defunct animal sanctuary without a second thought but was frozen like a deer in headlights over something as silly as a painted shadow.

"What are you thinking about so hard over here?" A deep voice interrupted her reverie.

"I think I need a therapist," she murmured in response before realizing who she was even talking to. "Hey, Marcus. How are you settling in?"

"Fine, thank you. And after all you've been through, I'd be more surprised if you didn't need a therapist."

"You know, I was joking when I said it but now that you mention it, I should probably look into that."

An awkward silence followed. Not that she could blame him. She wouldn't have known what to say to that, either.

"Do you know much about shadowing?" She asked before amending, "Of course you do. You're an artist. Let me rephrase that: Could you help me out with my daisies?"

"Absolutely," he answered without hesitation. "By help, do you mean teach you how or do it?"

She handed him her paint brush in response.

"I got you." His smile was warm, the kind that pulled a person in.

"Thank you." Nora melted with relief into a corner, happy to watch him turn her doodles into art. "So, what brings you to St. Augustine?"

His chuckle told her there was a story there. "My sister thought I should try my hand at making my art into a business. She says I'm too old to keep doing the starving artist thing."

"Funny. She's always trying to rein me in when I talk to her about new businesses."

"Don't you have, like, twelve of them or something?"

"Don't judge." Nora frowned briefly. "And I only own three. Wait, four. Yes. Four."

Marcus' bark of laughter was too infectious for Nora to be offended.

"Where were you doing the starving artist thing?"

"New Orleans."

"That sounds fun."

"It was. But Ivy is right. It was time to try something new, and Pru seems cool. I think I'll like it here." With a final flourish, he stepped back from the wall. "Is that better?"

"It's amazing, thank you." Nora smiled at the flowers. The transformation truly was amazing. It fascinated her how the smallest change could make such a difference. It reminded her of watching Bob Ross as a girl, thinking a painting was perfect and being worried when he said he was going to add just one more touch and then that touch was exactly what it needed.

August called for a food break, saving Nora from having to come up with something else to paint. She was picking at a salad and wondering if it would be rude to use her head injury as an excuse to go home when Lucca sat down beside her again. One look at his face told her what he was getting ready to say.

"No." She shoved a lettuce leaf in her mouth and gave him the sternest look she could muster with buttercrunch sticking out the corner of her mouth.

"You don't even know what I was going to say." His look was more petulant teen than feared mob boss.

Nora raised her eyebrows expectantly. "What were you going to say?"

"I really wish you'd reconsider—" he began, only to be cut off by Nora.

"No." She shoved the plate back, unable to pretend food held the remotest appeal. "Don't ask me why because I'll never be able to explain it, but I actually care what happens to you, Lucca. I'm still reeling from the loss of the *Manolia Jane*. I can't lose you, too."

"So, I rank with the boat?"

"You're a link to Uncle Walter."

"And nothing more?" He looked hurt. "I thought we were friends."

"You're a pain in my backside," she added.

"Wounded. I am wounded by your cruel words, Nora."

"Uh-huh." She sighed. "Give me one more day to see what I can turn up. If I'm still empty-handed by tomorrow night, I will consider it. We can meet for dinner to discuss where things stand."

"That's really more of a day and a half."

She raised one perfectly manicured eyebrow.

"Dinner tomorrow is good."

With no clue what to do next and one day to get one, Nora decided to stop by the marina on her way home. It frustrated her being so wholly out of the loop on this investigation. She imagined Raf would tell her that's the way it was supposed to be, but that felt like utter nonsense to her. Besides, as one of the owners at the marina, surely she was entitled to see surveillance video.

Having spent her day playing chase with Buck, Margo was sound asleep in her car seat by the time Nora pulled into the yacht club.

"Sorry girl. Just one stop and then we'll head home," Nora promised.

They were halfway across the parking lot when Nora noticed the well-dressed neighbor who gave her heebie-jeebies. Instinctively, she shortened Margo's leash. She couldn't say why; she just felt safer with the dog close. Nora tried to swing a wide arc around the unpleasant man, but he altered his course in concert with hers, ensuring the two crossed paths.

Nora offered a terse nod by way of greeting, intending to sidestep him.

"Nora Jones!" His tone was artificially bright. "It's a shame about Walter's boat."

"It is." She pressed her lips into a thin line, biting back a thousand less-appropriate responses.

"Of course, that's what happens when you let inexperienced sailors loose with a boat they have no business sailing."

"The *Magnolia Jane* was sabotaged," she informed him pertly, not sure why she felt the need to defend herself.

His eyebrows shot up. "Was it? That's too bad. Who on earth would do such a thing?"

"Who indeed." Nora's was a statement rather than a question as she pinned him with a pointed look. "I don't believe you've given me your name, though you seem to know mine well enough."

"I don't believe I have." His expression was smug. "You know that boat was mine, before your uncle stole her from me."

"My understanding is they got the boat in a government auction. Isn't that what happens when someone does something illegal? Maybe I'm wrong. We inexperienced sailors are so easily confused." She smiled sweetly at him before leaving him to scowl at her retreating back.

Nora took a deep breath as she opened the office door, resetting her mood so she could greet the young woman at the desk with a cheerful hello.

"Hey-a Miss Jones." The girl looked up from the crossword she was working on. "What's a five-letter word for 'tread heavily on'?"

Nora paused. "Tromp?"

The girl looked down for a moment before shaking her head. "Nope. Good guess, though. What can I help you with?"

"Ginny, do you have security footage from before my accident?"

"I gave everything we have to the sheriff's office."

"Is there a copy I could take a peek at?"

Ginny grinned. "Sure. How long do you need?"

"How much do you have?"

"We keep footage for two weeks."

"Can I see all of it?"

"That'll be too big to email. I can send you a link, though."

"That would be amazing, thank you." Nora turned to go before pausing and glancing back over her shoulder. "What about plods?"

The young woman's eyebrows knit together in confusion.

"Your crossword."

"Nah, the first letter is definitely a 't'. You were on the right track there."

Nora bit her lip and thought. "Tramp?"

After some scribbling, Ginny brightened. "That totally works!"

Nora nodded, satisfied. "Oh, hey, did you know my slip neighbor used to own the *Magnolia Jane*?"

"Harold?" Ginny scrunched her nose before catching herself and replacing her expression with a placid one. "I hadn't heard that. Small world, huh?"

"It is."

Nora mulled over the encounter at the yacht club as she navigated her way through traffic. She contemplated stopping for dinner on her way home, but she was so exhausted it felt insurmountable. Honestly, even eating felt like more effort than it was worth.

When she got home, she instantly changed into pajamas and settled on the couch with her laptop and a glass of orange juice. Margo finished her own dinner and climbed up next to Nora, pressing herself as close as possible.

Nora scratched the dog's ears absentmindedly as she watched the footage of people coming and going from the marina. It was impossible to know everyone and who should or should not be there, but she had to start somewhere.

She was fighting the urge to nod off when there was a knock at the door. She sighed; climbing out from under the dog and computer felt like way more effort than she wanted to exert at the moment.

"Nora?" Raf called from the other side of the door.

She closed her laptop and set it aside, not especially eager to fight with Rafael about involving herself in the investigation. When she opened the door, he held up a paper bag by way of greeting.

"A little birdie told me you haven't been eating much."

"Does that little birdie have wild hair and a penchant for snarky t-shirts?" Nora raised her eyebrows.

"I couldn't say," he answered. "Not without risking my life, anyway."

She chuckled, standing aside for him to enter. "What did you bring me?" She caught a whiff of something intriguing and her stomach rumbled in response.

"Street tacos."

"Ooh, nice. I'll get plates."

"Nah, you sit. I'll get plates."

Nora obliged, in part because she was curious how things would play out but mostly because the tacos smelled really good. The first bite confirmed that they tasted as good as they smelled. She closed her eyes and sighed.

"Does that mean I'm forgiven?" he asked.

She opened her eyes and glanced his way. "That means this is a damn fine taco. Forgiveness will require a conversation."

"A conversation?"

"Yes. Preferably one in which you tell me what's really going on here."

"I can't do that yet."

Nora frowned, her joy in the food somewhat diminished. "That's unfortunate. Still, thank you for the tacos."

He sat awkwardly for a moment and then asked, "Can I have one?"

She considered telling him no, but that felt a little bratty. Instead, she slid the bag his way.

"Thank you." He unwrapped a taco and hesitated. "Do you want to watch TV or something?"

She slid the remote his way, too, before settling further back on the couch. Now that she had some food in her belly, the pull of sleep was even stronger. She barely made it through the show's opening credits before she was tucked up under Rafael's arm, sound asleep.

Chapter Eight

NORA SNUGGLED CLOSER TO Rafael, inhaling deeply to savor the hints of sandalwood and bergamot, scents that brought her comfort because she associated them with him. His arm tightened around her, and she knew that he was awake, too. Sunbeams trickled through the curtains, entreating her to join the day. Somewhere in the night, they'd shifted positions and slept wrapped around each other on the couch.

Nora peeked over his shoulder to see Margo curled up in the chair opposite them, watching intently for signs of life. Too late, Nora closed her eyes and pretended to still be asleep. Margo saw through the ruse and crossed the distance between them with a single bound, resting her chin on Rafael's shoulder and slowly sticking her tongue out to tentatively lick Nora's face.

A chuckle rumbled in Rafael's chest. "I think the gig is up."

Nora sighed.

"You could ignore her," he suggested.

In response, Margo added a soft but piercing whine to her plea while increasing the force behind her kisses.

"I don't think so." Nora stretched. "She's very tenacious when it comes to breakfast."

Satisfied that Nora was appropriately motivated to move, Margo turned her attention to Rafael. He laughed and tucked his head in his arm to keep from French kissing the dog. "That's like a giraffe's tongue."

"How do you know what a giraffe's tongue is like?"

"How do you not? Have you never fed a giraffe?"

"Why would I have fed a giraffe?"

"We must rectify this," he resolved.

Nora couldn't respond, she was too busy laughing, trying to bury her head against Rafael to shield herself from the damp alarm clock that came in the form of Miss Margo's tongue.

"Would you like me to let her out?" he asked.

"Yes, please. I'll make her breakfast." Her voice was muffled against his neck. It took a moment for them to untangle, progress further hampered by Margo's help. "My hero!" Nora called after him as he led the gangly dog away. He waved in response.

Nora rolled off the couch and stretched before padding into the kitchen to get Margo's food out of the fridge. She wasn't sure how long this truce with Rafael would last, but she was enjoying it while it lingered.

"Do you want some coffee?" she asked, glancing his way as he joined her in the kitchen. From the scowl on his face as he looked at his phone, she had a sinking feeling that their peace would be short lived.

"Nora—" he paused, seeming to search for his next words. "James Byrd is out."

She paled. That wasn't even remotely what she'd been expecting him to say. She'd signed up for notifications about his status but had been so busy with everything, she still hadn't cleared out her inbox. The notice was probably buried in there somewhere.

"He got out two weeks ago."

"Before the accident?"

"The day before," he confirmed.

"So, it could have been him."

Rafael nodded briefly. "It's worth looking into. I'd clarify that it's worth the police looking into, but we both know I'd be wasting my breath."

"Coffee?" she asked again, sliding a cup his direction without waiting for a response.

"Thanks." He wrapped his hands around the mug but made no move to take a drink. Instead, he took a deep breath and caught her gaze with a look that pierced right through to her soul. "I don't suppose there's anything you'd like to tell me about Lucca Buccio skipping out on WITSEC?"

"Nothing I'd *like* to tell you." She knew her emphasis on the word like told him plenty.

"I see." His face was grim as he finally took a sip of his coffee.

"Some things aren't mine to tell, Raf."

"I just wish you trusted me enough to be honest."

At that, she frowned. "I haven't been dishonest. And that statement feels a bit hypocritical coming from you right now."

He bristled. "What's that supposed to mean?"

Nora pointed at his phone. "Are you ready to tell me why you spend most of your time scowling at that these days?"

She expected him to argue. To scowl more fiercely. To shut her down again. She didn't expect him to sink onto the barstool and hang his head. When he looked back up at her, there was an openness she hadn't seen from him in a while.

"I think I'm in trouble, Nora."

She silently reached out and took his hand, afraid that anything she might say would change his mind about opening up to her.

"You know my dad was a dirty cop—"

Nora wanted to interject that Lucca asserted otherwise but held her tongue, merely nodding to encourage him to continue.

"They said he was on the take... from Lucca Buccio."

"Oh." Nora came around the counter to sink onto a stool beside Rafael. "So, my unique relationship with Lucca probably doesn't look so good for you."

"Not especially, no."

"Raf, I'm so sorry."

"I've been placed under investigation."

"For what?"

"Inappropriate relationships with questionable people."

"Oh," she said again, the reality of his words sinking in. She might cost Rafael his job.

"That's only officially, though." He reached over and put his arm around her, kissing her on top of the head before resting his cheek on her. "I think it has more to do with the fact that I testified against someone in a misconduct hearing last month. The officer lost his job, but he still has friends on the force."

"But I gave them what they needed to come after you. It's still my fault. If you'd never met me, you would have been untouchable."

"Nobody is untouchable," he countered. "And if I'd never met you, my life would be incredibly dull. I'll take the colorful version of my world anytime, even if it is more complicated."

"I thought you were getting ready to break up with me." Nora didn't know why she brought that up. Her silly anxieties were clearly not as important as him potentially losing his job, or worse.

"I definitely have no intention of breaking up with you. You're stuck with me Nora Jones. Though you might not want me if I'm an unemployed lay about."

"Are you forgetting that you own shares of an honest-to-God treasure, Raf? Even if you stopped being a police officer, you'd still have a job. Or income, I suppose would be the more accurate way to say it."

"I can't see myself being content with passive income. Besides, being a police officer was about more than a job."

"It was restoring your family's name," she surmised, her voice soft.

"Maybe I'm trying to fix something that can't be fixed. Maybe the Medero name is just cursed."

"Medero is a good name. Maybe it can be restored, maybe it can't. But that doesn't change the man you are, the man I know you to be. You keep doing what you believe is right and the truth will eventually find its way to the surface, even if it's not when and how we'd like it to." Nora wanted to wrap herself around him and make it all go away. Was it possible for love to wash away generations of hurt? She wasn't sure, but she was willing to try.

"Thank you." He kissed the top of her head again before straightening. "Like it or not, I should probably get to work."

"Call if you want to meet for lunch, or if you need to talk."

"I will," he promised. "What's in store for your day? Or am I better off not knowing?"

Nora smiled. "I'm wedding dress shopping with August. And I need to finish watching surveillance footage from the yacht club."

Rafael chuckled. "I guess I'm glad to see it's not just me you second guess."

"I do not second guess you." She swatted at him. "But I don't think anyone is investigating my case."

"Do you want me to see what I can find out?"

"No, thank you. Given everything you have on your plate, it's probably best if you don't."

"Do you want to grab dinner?" he asked.

"I would love to, but I have plans."

"Yeah? With who?" His tone was conversational, but Nora still hesitated. "Ah, *that* I'm better off not knowing," he surmised.

She patted his leg and kissed his cheek before heading off to get ready for her day. Not that her day was going to be too terribly exciting. At least not the morning, which mostly consisted of watching grainy video of random strangers coming and going from the marina while hoping something—anything—would give her a clue as to what happened to her beloved boat.

When the morning proved a bust, Nora tucked her laptop away and rounded up Margo to go meet August at Buena Onda Café for lunch before they went dress shopping. Nora couldn't foresee going entirely vegan like August and Leo, but she had to admit she enjoyed the little family-run café's mushroom melt sandwich, and it was possible she was addicted to their ginger mint lemonade.

Per usual, Nora arrived first and snagged one of the three tables on the sidewalk while she waited. August blew in like a summer storm, looking a bit frazzled. She wore an orange patchwork skirt that was so long her turquoise toenails barely peeked out from the hem and a cream-colored t-shirt with orange print that read, "I'm sorry I'm late. I saw a dog."

A smile tugged the corner of Nora's mouth as she hugged her friend hello. "Do you want to watch Margo while I snag our lunch?" she asked.

August waved her off. "Nah, you sit. I'll grab the food. Do you want your usual?"

"Absolutely." Nora settled back into her seat and waited for August to reappear with their sandwiches.

"So—" August began as she settled in her seat once their food arrived. "Any news on the investigation?"

"Nothing much." Nora took a bit of her lunch and gave herself a moment to enjoy the flavors exploding on her tastebuds before setting the sandwich down and leaning forward to fill August in on where things stood thus far. She left out Rafael's trouble at work, even if a part of her deeply wanted to confide in her friend and ask for guidance. It felt like betraying his newly won trust, though, so she held her tongue.

"I wouldn't call James Byrd being out of prison nothing much." August frowned and took a sip of her lemonade. "He certainly has reason to get payback."

"Hey!" Nora straightened. "He's the one who robbed me."

August held her hands up in surrender. "I know, I know. But he doesn't strike me as the type to have much personal accountability."

"Point taken," Nora conceded. "I have a bad feeling about Harold, the creepy neighbor."

"What is it with you and neighbors?" August smirked.

"You're all kinds of saucy today, aren't you?"

August shrugged. "Pre-wedding nerves."

"We need to get this wedding planned so you stop using that as an excuse."

"Don't worry." August patted her hand. "I'll find another."

Nora laughed and shook her head. "I'm sure you will."

They finished their lunches and took Margo for a walk before hitting a few of the bridal shops in town. After the third shop, August declared the day a bust. Nora couldn't be sure if she hadn't seen anything she liked or hadn't seen anything she could afford, but she didn't push the issue. Besides, she was tired and still needed to check in on the bookstore before her dinner with Lucca. And she wanted to swing by to see if Mykal might want to go to dinner with them. The two of them still had an uneasy relationship, but she figured it wouldn't hurt to ask.

As she made her way through the crowded tourist district, Nora soaked in the ambience of the bustling street. She liked the vibe of the place she now called home. It was an eclectic mix of history and tourist kitsch. She didn't think she'd ever stop marveling over the variety of shops that bordered hers. She waved at Samara, the owner of The Cauldron on her way by, making a mental note to pop in and say a proper hello soon. She picked up the pace when she noticed Jerry was working on a window display. He was nice enough, but she didn't have the 40 minutes a quick hello would cost her. Maybe August was right; maybe Nora was a terrible neighbor. Setting that thought aside as clear fallacy, she smiled as the bell above the door tinkled a merry hello when she walked into Worth Their Salt.

There was just something about this bookstore that would always feel like home, no matter how many businesses she accrued in her odd little empire. She'd gone to the trouble of getting an actual office to work out of but never seemed to use it, preferring the energy at this little shop. A sense of nostalgia swept through her, and she suddenly missed the days of her and Pru and August running this place together.

Reginald smiled at her from behind the counter, and it occurred to Nora that there was a lot to miss if time stood still, no matter how badly we might long for the moments that had passed.

"How are you feeling, Miss Nora?" he asked.

"Much better," she answered. "I can't thank you enough for stepping up so much with me out." Nora knew words were nice but paying employees what they were worth was nicer, so she'd already talked to Ivy about giving Reginald a pay bump. "How are things here at the store?"

"Pretty quiet today. We had an author reach out about doing a book signing; I said I would check with you."

"Local author?"

Reginald nodded.

"Are they any good?"

"Not my particular genre, but they seem well rated."

"Send me a link, if you don't mind, but that should be fine." Nora chatted with Reginald for a few more minutes, promising to take a look at the author and to teach him how to set up events so he could make those judgment calls himself before heading back to her office to sort through work emails before they got too out of hand. As predicted, the email warning her of James Byrd's release was buried in between an invoice and a sale announcement from her favorite brand. Inwardly, she kicked herself for not setting a filter to flag the message, though she certainly hadn't envisioned life getting as away from her as it had the last couple of weeks.

She also had an email from Gregory with an inventory of the items found in the forward section of the ship. She could tell from his tone it was an amazing find, though the words themselves meant little to her. She was glad to have found a replacement for Arin Lancaster to oversee the expedition. The new archaeologist had come highly recommended and would know how best to process the items they were pulling off the ocean floor—and how to navigate the murky waters of who owned what. It bothered Nora to not have a better sense of the inner workings of a business she owned, but not so much that she was willing to put in the time required to get up to speed. So, she replied to Gregory's email with an enthusiasm she didn't wholly feel and forwarded the message to someone more qualified to actually do something useful with the information.

The email from Ivy with a new list of potential Hummingbird Foundation recipients was a welcome one, though her brain couldn't seem to process the attached applications. Knowing it would slip through the cracks if she simply closed the email, Nora sacrificed a tree to print the applications off, telling herself it was a good project to tackle while curled up on her couch with Margo.

Once her inbox was tamed, she opened up the surveillance video file she'd saved to the cloud and let it play while she dialed Mykal to invite her to dinner.

As it turns out, Mykal was already climbing the walls since nobody would allow her to do anything, insisting she needed rest to properly heal. While Nora thought that was a fair point, given that Mykal had only recently been released from the hospital, she could also empathize with the woman's situation, so she agreed to swing by to pick her up on her way to the restaurant.

Nora glanced at her phone to end the call and nearly missed it, the guy in a hoodie slinking across the screen. A hoodie in Florida this time of year was definitely unusual. She couldn't quite make out the logo but froze the image to grab a screenshot. Maybe someone with more tech savvy than her could clean it up a bit. The hooded man was off-screen for a bit before slinking back the way he came. He wasn't off camera long enough to have gone out on a boat, which raised Nora's hackles all the more.

Still mulling over the mystery man on the screen, Nora packed up her stuff and said her goodbyes to Reginald before heading over to Mykal's house. She would arrive a few minutes early, but didn't really have enough time to go do anything else and figured early was better than late. As she pulled onto Mykal's street, she noticed a man leaving her friend's building. He was striking even from a distance—the epitome of tall, dark, and handsome. Nora wondered if she'd just caught a glimpse of "trouble with a capital 'T'" but wasn't about to ask, even though the question was burning a hole in her tongue as she watched her friend lock her door and drop her keys into her purse.

"That's a cute bag," Nora commented instead.

"Thanks! I got it at Marci's shop. It's just around the corner from us."

"I'll have to check it out." Nora was pretty sure she could spend an entire day meandering in and out of shops and not make it to see all of their neighbors in the historic district.

It was nearly an hour out to the seafood joint situated on the St John's River in Palatka, but the view was lovely, and Nora was reasonably sure they wouldn't run into anyone there who'd recognize Lucca. Not that anyone would recognize this Steve Irwin wannabe as the former mob boss for the reigning crime family in St Augustine, an outfit made all the more amusing by the fact that the place they had chosen to eat was known as gator landing.

It was a pleasant enough dinner, albeit a bit frustrating because Lucca was so single-mindedly fixated on his theory and unwilling to even hear Nora out or glance at the screenshot she tried to show him of the man she was increasingly convinced was the saboteur.

"You're not going to let this go until we rule it out as a possibility, are you?" Nora gave up all pretense of having an appetite and set down her fork.

"Then I'll look into it," Mykal volunteered.

Lucca shook his head. "That's the exact opposite of my intention in coming here."

"I'm not going to let you do it—they will kill you if they find out where you are," she reminded him.

"I still have friends," he argued.

"So you think. You can't be sure where loyalties lie," Nora said.

Lucca placed a hand over his heart. "Again, you wound me with your words."

Nora refused to budge. "Better to wound you with words than watch you die."

"She's right," Mykal added. "Besides, I have someone I can ask."

Lucca's eyebrows shot up the question he was dying to ask written all over his face.

Nora held up a hand to stay what would surely be a fight. "I'll go with her. We'll be careful. You, sir, need to go back to reptile wrangling and lay low."

Lucca grumbled under his breath like a sullen teenager. "I'm no good at all tucked away on that farm. I might as well have stayed gone."

Nora raised her eyebrows pointedly at him but let it drop. Rafael was not going to be happy about this.

Chapter Nine

AS SHE GOT DRESSED the next morning, Nora mulled over how she'd go about fulfilling her promise to Lucca without putting Rafael's career in further danger. She was no closer to the answer by the time she had Margo walked and loaded into the car, so she decided the only obvious thing to do was get breakfast. There are very few things in life that can't be fixed by waffles.

Her selection of restaurants was somewhat limited by the ever-present greyhound at her side, but it was a small price to pay. Besides, she preferred to eat outside, anyway. In Nora's opinion, every meal was made better with a bit of sunshine and a fresh breeze, and waffles were no exception. She'd ordered her breakfast and doctored her coffee to perfection, holding the cup just below her lips to ascertain if it was cool enough to take that first delectable sip when the tension in Margo's body alerted her to a man approaching her table.

Her stomach tightened with dread as recognition dawned. His hair was grayer, his body leaner, but it was unmistakably Jame Byrd approaching her table. Prison had done nothing to help the scowl of distaste he wore. She wondered briefly if that was his general demeanor or one that he reserved for her.

It was tempting to ignore him, hoping the breeze would carry him away like a bad stench. But Nora supposed the longer she took to acknowledge him, the longer he would linger and more agitated he would become.

She set her coffee down and met his gaze unflinchingly. "Hello, James."

"That's Captain Byrd to you, Nora."

She arched an eyebrow. "Oh? Have you acquired a new ship then?" She knew the answer but wasn't in the mood to play nice. It was his fault for depriving her of coffee, really.

From his glare and unintelligible grumble, she surmised the answer was no.

"Is a captain without a ship still a captain?" She wondered aloud before taking a sip of her coffee with an outward calm she did not feel. "Besides, you just called me Nora. Clearly, we're on a first name basis. So, what can I help you with, James?"

"I heard about your little mishap."

"Seems like half the town has."

"Seems like that's what you get for always sticking your nose where it don't belong." He emphasized the first two words in a mimicking way that reminded her of a schoolyard bully.

"Why James, are you threatening me? Or was that an admission of guilt? I wonder what your probation officer would say if they learned about this conversation." She willed her hands to not shake.

"Like I said, always sticking your nose where it don't belong."

"I didn't seek you out—you approached me. I'm so sorry your mother didn't love you enough to teach you about personal accountability."

At that, his face reddened, and Nora thought perhaps his mother was, in fact, the reason for his disdain for women. She was more concerned with her immediate safety and the that her waffles would be arriving soon, though.

"How about this?" She laid a hand on Margo's back, drawing courage from the dog's presence. "How about you stay away from me and mine and I leave you alone? I'd be more than happy to pretend you don't exist if you'd extend me the same courtesy."

Hatred oozed from his eyes as he growled. "You uppity—"

Nora held up a hand to stop what was coming next. "Think very carefully about your next words, James. We're in a public place with security cameras. One more word and I will take it as a threat and act accordingly. If you don't want to end up back in jail, I suggest you turn and walk away."

Margo added a well-timed growl of her own to the conversation, and Nora decided right then and there she was splitting her bacon with the dog.

Inwardly, Nora wanted nothing more than to run straight to Rafael to bury her head in his shoulder and let him wrap his arms around her to protect her from the boogey men of this world. Outwardly, she met James Byrd's gaze steadily in a staring contest that seemed to drag on for ages before he let out a string of expletives as he turned and stormed away.

Nora let out the breath she didn't realize she'd been holding and took a steadying sip of her coffee. She wondered what exactly he'd hoped to accomplish by harassing her at breakfast. Had he followed her here, or was it a chance encounter? Had he been the one to sink the *Magnolia Jane* and crashing in on her breakfast had been his chance to gloat? Would the encounter be enough to convince Lucca that there were suspects aplenty without involving the mob? She doubted it but resolved herself to try to get him to drop it once last time before she made things any harder for Raf at work by having a one-on-one with yet another crime boss.

For the first time in her life, Nora was glad the kitchen took forever to prepare her food. It gave her time to calm down before her breakfast arrived. If James Byrd ruined her waffles, she might actually riot. Maybe it was being fresh off a brain injury, but Nora felt off-kilter. Her usual calm curiosity eluded her and dang it, she needed comfort food.

At long last, her breakfast was served. Nora broke off a small piece of the bacon and offered it to Margo as payment for so perfectly punctuating her threat to the bully who'd tried to ruin their morning. Then she spread butter on her waffles, enjoying the way the golden yellow melted into each divot before burying it with a generous helping of syrup.

The first bite had nearly made it to her mouth when she noticed a dapper-looking older gentleman in a suit decidedly walking her way. He was flanked by two gorillas. Even though they'd never met, Nora had a sinking feeling that she knew exactly who this was: Enzo DiLella, the new don. She eyed the forkful of syrupy goodness longingly before setting down her utensil and forcing a smile at the man's greeting.

Nora didn't have to wonder long what he was there for. After the briefest exchange of pleasantries, he got right to the point.

"Ms. Jones, I have no desire to resume my predecessor's quarrel with you. Nor am I inclined to follow in Lucca Buccio's footsteps to forge a friendship, no matter how interesting a woman you may be."

Nora was almost afraid to breathe. "So where does that leave us, then?"

"I propose we ignore each other."

"That seems rather—" Nora searched for the word. "—reasonable of you."

"If you're implying that I could just kill you and be done with it, you're not wrong."

He didn't mince words. Nora had to give him that much.

"But someone I trust has made a compelling argument for why that would ultimately be more trouble than it's worth."

Nora wondered who she had to thank for her life. Regardless, she was grateful. Still, she felt it wise to put some parameters on their uneasy truce. "You do know that even if I agree to ignore you, that doesn't mean I can keep Rafael from coming after you if he catches a case that you're involved in."

"I suppose we'll just cross that bridge when we come to it, then. Won't we?"

"I suppose we will." Nora paused before musing. "The suspect list for *Janey*'s saboteur is certainly narrowing."

"I assume you're referring to the unfortunate incident with your boat?" He didn't wait for confirmation before continuing. "For that, Ms. Jones, I suggest you look on the other side of the law."

Nora had never been punched, but she suspected it felt something like what she was currently experiencing. Her breath left in a forceable whoosh, and it took a moment for her to regain the ability to speak. When she did, she hoped her voice sounded calmer than she felt. "That's an interesting statement. Is it fueled by anything in particular?"

"Merely an observation. I understand Detective Medero isn't exactly popular among his peers of late."

Nora pursed her lips in thought. "Trying to kill me seems a bit drastic of a response, though."

Enzo chuckled, raising his eyebrows and hands as if to say he didn't know. "Possibly, but it's obvious the detective loves you, and he is exceedingly unpopular. I'm sure you've heard of the blue wall of silence. He broke the code. That won't be taken lightly."

"I'll take that under advisement." Nora nodded her head slightly. "Thank you."

"You're welcome." He nodded once in return. "And Ms. Jones—," he paused.

She raised her eyebrows in question.

"Your new employee at that little animal farm of yours... I hear he bears a striking resemblance to a mutual friend."

"They do say everyone has a doppelganger out there in the universe."

"So, you're saying it's not him?"

"I'm saying our mutual acquaintance is terrified of snakes. He'd make a terrible choice for a reptile keeper, don't you think?"

At that, a smile ticked at the corner of his mouth. He turned and left without so much as a farewell, leaving Nora to stare at her now-soggy waffles, her stomach rumbling and her mind a jumble. The morning had not gone as planned, not even a little.

Chapter Ten

NORA TRIED TO GO about her day. If she was a bit distracted during Reginald's training session, he was kind enough not to mention it. Midway through the morning, she texted Rafael and asked him to meet her for lunch. He replied back that he'd love to but hadn't planned on taking a lunch. She replied that he needed to eat, and they needed to talk, so he promised to meet her at their favorite beachside café at 12:30. After having missed breakfast, that felt impossibly far away, but she was such a bundle of nerves, she couldn't promise her stomach wouldn't revolt if she tried to eat anyway.

When she was fairly confident Reginald had everything that he needed to start setting up events for the store, she left him to it and went back to her office to call August to warn her that Lucca's presence had been discovered.

"Do you think he believed you that it wasn't Lucca?" August asked after Nora finished relaying the conversation.

"Not for a second," Nora admitted. "But he seemed amused at the idea of Lucca doomed to a life of tending to snakes, so he might just leave him to his purgatory."

"A chance I'd be a little more willing to take if I didn't have a daughter living here."

"That's absolutely reasonable. I'll talk to Lucca to see if we can find somewhere else for him to go."

"Let me think about it a bit. We might be able to sort something out. No need to rush into anything," August said before switching gears. "Hey, we're having a luncheon here on Saturday. Can you make it?"

"I think so. I'll talk to Raf at lunch to be sure we don't have plans."

"Let me rephrase that. We're having a luncheon on Saturday, and you and Rafael will be here at 11:30."

Nora laughed. "Good to know. I'll inform Raf."

"Thank you. And we'll sort out the Lucca thing after that."

"You don't think the danger might be more imminent?"

"I'll talk to Leo about beefing up security. We'll be okay."

Nora couldn't place her finger on it, but there was something odd about the entire conversation. Perhaps she'd have pestered August to find out what was off if her own brain wasn't already so preoccupied with that she was going to say to Rafael at lunch.

She still hadn't entirely worked that out by the time she found herself sitting across from him, waiting for her chicken sandwich to be delivered. So, she started with the easier topic.

"Hopefully you're free on Saturday because August has strongly requested our presence out at the farm for lunch that day."

He raised an eyebrow, amusement etched on his face. "Strongly requested?"

"It was more of a decree."

"They're not going to make us eat vegan food, are they?"

"Do you want me to smuggle in some bacon in my purse?"

"Is that an option?"

"Emergency bacon?" Nora chuckled. "Sure, we can make that happen."

"Admit it, you want emergency bacon, too." His smile was altogether charming.

"I will admit no such thing."

"But you can't deny it, either, because we both know that would be a lie."

"Well, I mean, if it's already there, it would be a shame to waste it," Nora conceded.

"I wonder if the dogs will rat you out..." Rafael let out the first real laugh Nora had seen from him in weeks. "I'm sorry, I can just imagine you being swarmed by a pack of dogs all day because you have a stash of bacon in your purse."

"You're right. We'll need an airtight container."

"You always think two steps ahead, Nora. It's one of the many reasons I love you."

Nora flushed at the compliment. Even if the conversation was ridiculous, the compliment was genuine, and it meant the world coming from him. She could think of few people she respected more.

"Raf, I have to tell you, I had an unexpected visitor at breakfast. Two of them, actually—" Nora dove into a recounting of her failed attempt at waffles before she could lose her nerve. All traces of laughter left Rafael's face as he absorbed her words.

He sat in silence for a moment after she finished talking. She could almost see the wheels turning in his head as he processed her words. Finally, he took her hands in his and looked her straight in the eye. "I am so deeply sorry that there is even the slightest chance that your case isn't being investigated because of me—or worse, someone did this to you to get to me. And James Byrd approaching you at breakfast terrifies me. It might be worth filing a temporary protective order."

"Would it do me any good?"

"There might be a few bad elements in the force—there are in any group—but there are good people, too. I have to believe that."

"But isn't a restraining order only good if someone honors it?"

"To a point, but it gives police a reason to arrest him if he does approach you."

Nora chewed her lip as she considered. "Does that impact his probation? I told him I'd live and let live."

Rafael shook his head. "It only impacts it if he violates the TPO. And while I appreciate you being a woman of your word, I care more that you stay alive."

"I'll think about it," she promised.

He nodded, letting the subject drop as their server delivered their food. The couple settled into silence as they ate. It's possible he'd heard her stomach rumbling and realized she needed food before she got hangry. Her brain always worked better when it had been properly fed.

It wasn't until Nora finally pushed her plate back, certain she couldn't take one more bite, that Rafael finally circled back to more serious matters. "Everything in me wants to take the rest of the day off, to not let you out of my sight again until we solve this thing together. But I think I'd be of more use in the office, seeing what I can learn from there."

"That makes sense," Nora agreed. If only to herself, she had to admit that the notion of them solving this thing together was a welcome one. She liked working with Rafael. Something about the way his brain worked made hers more effective, too.

"I do think I feel a summer cold coming on, though," he added with a fake cough. "I'll probably have to call in sick tomorrow."

"That's too bad." Nora grinned at his antics, feeling more relief than she was prepared to admit.

"Should I swing by tonight after work? We can grab some takeout and make a plan of attack?"

"I'd like that very much." She impulsively leaned forward to kiss him. "Thank you."

"A public display of affection? What is this world coming to?" he teased, earning a light swat on his arm.

"Just for that, you get to pick up dinner on your way."

"Duly noted. And to show I'm properly contrite, I'll even pick up the check for lunch." He offered his credit card to the server, his eyes dancing with amusement as he watched her mouth twist as she bit back a retort.

Even if she was no closer to answers, Nora's heart felt lighter by the time the tinkling bell above the door at Worth Their Salt Books greeted her. She and Raf were a team again; things would be fine—she was certain of it.

Her mind was so busy turning over the events of the day that she nearly bumped into Bryan as she came through the door.

"Nora! There you are. I'd nearly given up on you."

"Hey, Bryan. I was just at lunch with my boyfriend." Nora felt the need to slip it into conversation that she had a boyfriend. "What's up?"

"I was just popping by to check in and see how you're doing."

"Much better, thank you."

"Any updates on what caused the accident?"

She shook her head in frustration. "No, we're no closer to figuring out who sabotaged the boat."

"So, it was sabotage? You're sure, then?"

"That much they *can* tell me." It was difficult to keep the irritation out of her voice.

"Wow. That's scary." He shook his head in sympathy. "And no idea who did it?"

"Not a one, but I'm sure they'll get to the bottom of it soon." She forced a brightness she didn't feel.

"I bet they will," he agreed. "Oh, hey, how's the other girl who was in the boat with you?"

"Mykal? She's doing much better, thank you. I'll tell her you asked about her."

"Yeah, you do that."

There was an awkward pause. Nora wasn't sure if it was the brain injury or if she was on overload from the day, but she had no ability to make small talk. Just as she opened her mouth to make her excuses, he saved her from having to.

"I guess I should go. I'll see you around." He gave her a cheerful smile and a wave.

"Yeah, see you around." She waved back before heading to her office to sift through the mountain of email that had accumulated.

There was an email from Gregory broaching the topic she'd so diligently been avoiding—the sale of the salvage business. In it, he asked if she'd be willing to sell the business sooner than planned if she retained a percentage of the profits from the current project. It was a fair offer, and Nora had no desire to stay in the recovery business, but agreeing to sell a piece of Walter's legacy so fresh off losing the *Magnolia Jane* felt wrong.

Rather than leave him hanging, she replied that it sounded like a reasonable offer and asked for a few days to run the numbers and think. She almost said to run it by Ivy, but then thought better of it. Asking Ivy to weigh in on that decision wasn't fair. Besides, it was Raf's opinion that mattered most. And she knew what he'd say: Sell the business. So really, she was just buying time. Time to process. Time to come to terms with yet more change. Maybe even time to grieve.

Her desire to work soured, she closed her email and called Mykal to fill her in on the morning's conversation. Whoever her friend's contact was on the inside, they were clearly well connected. It hadn't taken long at all for Mykal's inquiries to result in an in-person visit.

Mykal let out a low whistle. "That's quite the morning. At least now we know it doesn't have anything to do with Lucca."

"How do you interpret his response to my new employee at Quirkiosities?" Nora asked.

"I think he's safe, but I don't think he should push it. If he shows his face in town, it won't go over well."

Nora had the distinct impression Mykal was much more plugged into that whole scene than she let on, but she let it go. "Our rescuer came by the shop today. Wanted to check on how we're doing."

"I still haven't met this guy," Mykal said.

"He's nice. A bit attentive, but nice."

"What do you make of this luncheon August is having on Saturday?" Mykal asked. "Is it just me, or was she awfully insistent we all be there?"

"It wasn't just you," Nora assured her. "It definitely feels like something is up."

"Maybe she's pregnant."

Nora opened her mouth to disagree but paused. It wasn't out of the realm of possibility. Maybe she was gathering everyone for an announcement. "Okay, now I'm going to struggle not to get my hopes up."

"You know, if you want a baby, I'm sure Rafael would oblige."

"Goodness no; I don't want a baby of my own. I don't need that kind of responsibility. I just want to spoil someone else's."

"Sound logical." Mykal laughed. "I guess we'll find out on Saturday."

"Suddenly that feels very far away."

"It's Wednesday. I think you'll make it."

"And to think, there was a time when I wanted to be friends with you," Nora teased.

After a round of good-natured goodbyes, Nora was left with her emails, which had shockingly not answered themselves while she was on the phone. With a sigh, she went back to it until the clock told her she could respectably call it a day.

By the time she headed home, she wasn't in the best of moods. So much so that she even debated calling Rafael to cancel dinner. When she turned down her street, she realized it was too late to cancel—Rafael's Tahoe was parked in her driveway. Recognizing the car, Margo practically vibrated with the anticipation of seeing one of her favorite people.

The instant Nora let the dog off her leash, she took off through the house in proper zoomie-mode, though Nora's attention was on the candles lit throughout and the aroma of garlic that greeted her at the door.

If she lived to be 100, Nora was convinced she'd never see anything as beautiful as Rafael standing in her kitchen doorway, an apron over his suit, offering her a glass of wine with a look on contrition on his face.

"I'm sorry."

She raised her eyebrows as she accepted the offering. "For anything in particular? You didn't just set fire to the kitchen, did you?"

His chuckle was rueful. "Your kitchen is safe. I've just been doing a lot of thinking. I think I've let my priorities get out of whack."

She didn't want to risk shutting him down, so she took a sip of her wine and watched him as he figured out what he wanted to say next.

"I based my entire career on a desire to prove they were wrong about my dad. Or that I wasn't him." He ran a hand through his hair and let out a wry laugh. "To be honest, I don't even know who 'they' are, who I was trying to convince or why I cared."

"You're a good cop. A good man." Nora instinctively reached out to take his hand in her own.

"Thank you. And I love being a cop. But I don't know that I love everything it entails. How many times have I tried to keep you from working a case just to keep the peace at the office? Shouldn't finding the truth of a matter benefit us both?"

"I understand that we have laws for a reason."

A look of amusement flickered in his eyes. "There is some humor to us arguing each other's point of view now."

"Or maybe I was just listening better than you realized."

"Maybe I was, too." Rafael reached out to stroke her cheek with his thumb.

Nora's breath caught in her throat at the whisper of a touch. Feelings stirred that made it much more difficult to formulate coherent sentences. "What are you saying? Do you want to quit your job?"

"No. Yes. I don't know. Maybe."

"What would you do if you resigned?"

"I haven't figured that part out yet. I know I have income from the salvage find, but I don't see myself being content with passive income," he said.

"True, but having that income buys you the time to figure it out."

"Before I do anything, I think we need to use my badge to figure out what happened to the *Magnolia Jane*. Or, more importantly, who tried to kill you."

"Maybe they didn't mean to kill me. Maybe they just wanted to destroy *Janey*."

"Unless they were sitting and watching the boat sink, stranding you in the middle of the bay with no boat had a pretty good shot of killing you," Rafael argued. "But in keeping with that line of thinking, who would want to harm the boat but not necessarily you?"

"Harold," Nora answered without missing a beat. "The creepy neighbor down at the marina."

"What is it with you and neighbors?" he asked, earning a look of irritation from Nora.

"I do not have a thing with neighbors. He used to own *Janey*. He resented losing her in a government auction."

"A government auction?" Rafael's eyebrows shot up. "Are we sure she wasn't used in smuggling? That could tie her back to the mafia."

"They say they aren't involved."

"And the mob is known for their honesty." His tone was wry.

"I don't know; they kind of are. I don't think they'd be shy about owning up to it if they wanted me dead or just wanted their boat out of the picture."

"Possibly." He didn't seem convinced. "But we can add Harold to our suspect list if it will make you feel better."

"It will."

"So tomorrow we need to check out Harold the creepy neighbor, James Byrd... who else?"

"Any leads on your end?"

"Not really. If someone on the force did it, they're doing a great job keeping it under wraps. I get the feeling they aren't killing themselves to investigate because of your tie to me, but I don't think it goes farther than that. I've asked a couple of people I trust to keep their ears open for us, though."

"Shall we reserve that as a possibility but not pursue it for now?" Nora suggested.

Rafael nodded. "Sounds reasonable to me. And I'm willing to deprioritize the mafia theory but not willing to write it off just yet."

"Well, at least that gives us somewhere to focus our energy tomorrow," Nora sighed and sank onto a barstool at the counter.

"Yes, tomorrow. Tonight, let's focus our energy on dinner. And then a massage."

"A massage?" Nora repeated, unsure if she'd heard him correctly.

"I happen to be a very good masseur," he informed her.

"And you're just now sharing this information?"

Rafael gave her a look that was adorably contrite. "Did I mention my priorities have been off?"

"It did come up, yes."

He sat a plate of mouthwatering pasta in front of her. "Consider this step one of me rectifying the error."

"And the massage is step two?"

"It is."

"Nice." Nora twirled some angel hair pasta on her fork, a sigh escaping at the first bite. She could get on board with this new version of Rafael.

The next morning, they took their time puttering through making coffee and breakfast. Nora still felt happy and relaxed from the massage the night before. She considered suggesting a new career for Raf as a masseur but wasn't inclined to share his talents with the world.

"Before we head out, could we hang our pictures?" Nora asked once they were dressed.

"You know, I thought about doing that last night before you got home, as a surprise, but it occurred to me that you might have ideas about where you wanted them."

"You know me, I always have thoughts." Nora was self-aware enough to admit she could be a touch particular at times.

Raf gave her a grin that melted her. "I love your thoughts. Don't ever change."

Nora did wonder if he was reconsidering that sentiment by the time they finally had the pictures hung just right. Still, it made her heart happy to have something so thoroughly them hanging in her dining room.

When they finally got out of the house, their first stop was James Byrd's probation officer. He was a slender man with thinning hair that looked to be in desperate need of a wash. Nora couldn't help noting that his clothes looked like they could use a wash as well. His expression clearly stated that he would rather be anywhere other than in the drab brown office he currently found himself in. Nora couldn't say she blamed him. She'd rather be anywhere else, too.

Rafael leaned over and whispered in her ear. "Stop making that face."

"This is my face. I don't know how to make another one," she whispered back before plastering a smile on.

"Thanks for making the time to see us today, Seth." Rafael took control of the conversation. "We just have a few quick questions for you; we don't want to take up too much of your time.

"Sure, sure. You said you wanted to talk about James Byrd?"

"We do. It's our understanding he was released a few weeks ago."

The other man checked the file in front of him before nodding the affirmative.

"I don't suppose you happen to know his whereabouts on the 25th?" Rafael asked.

Seth shook his head. "Can't say that I do; we don't keep tabs on the guys 24/7. Though my guess would be work. He got a job at a landscape company. He usually works every day but Sunday."

"What about 2 a.m. on the 24th?" Nora interjected, earning a look of surprise from Rafael.

"Two in the morning on the 24th? Actually, I do. He was in the hospital."

"The hospital?" Nora blinked, thinking surely she misheard the man.

"The emergency room, to be precise. He was in a car accident over on I-95. Just minor bumps and bruises, but he checked himself into the ER over at Flagler as a precaution. The officer who took his statement called me the next morning to let me know one of mine was involved."

Deflated, Nora thanked the man, listening with only half an ear as he and Rafael finished their conversation. Once the couple was alone in the car, Rafael turned to Nora, his expression clearly asking the question before he could verbalize it.

"The surveillance videos from the marina," Nora explained. "There was a man in a hoodie there in the middle of the night. Not long enough for a boat ride, but too long to be lost. I think that's who sabotaged my boat."

"I'd ask why you didn't tell me this sooner, but we haven't exactly been communicating well lately, so I'll chalk it up to that."

Nora gave a half shrug, declining to mention that it really was his fault she'd started leaving him out of the loop.

"Can I see the video?"

"Sure." Nora pulled her phone out of her purse, pulling up the clip she'd saved for easy access and forwarding it to Raf's email.

He watched it in silence, his brow furrowed. When the clip was done, he looked up at Nora. "I think you're right. This is our guy. If we could make out that logo on his hoodie, I'd bet we'd be a lot closer to the truth."

"That's what I was thinking. I was tempted to ask Pru to take a look. She might be able to recreate it for me."

"Possibly, but I know someone at work who definitely can—someone I trust, I promise."

"Okay," Nora nodded, hope swelling in her chest. For the first time in weeks, she felt like she was finally getting somewhere. But then, good things happened when she and Rafael Medero put their heads together. They always did.

Chapter Eleven

NORA AND RAFAEL HAD ended their day of sleuthing with a stop by the marina in hopes of talking to Harold. When he hadn't been there, they'd left word with Ginny they were looking to have a chat with him. The next day, he'd pulled up anchor and left, solidifying in Nora's mind that the creepy neighbor was the number one suspect. Rafael had argued that a hoodie didn't seem the guy's style. And while Nora had to concede as much, she also argued that made it a perfect disguise.

By the time Nora dressed for August's mystery luncheon on Saturday, they still hadn't heard back from the digital artist who was supposed to be recreating the logo. Nora had the feeling that even among the people they considered allies, her case was low on the priority list. But then, maybe there'd been a crime spree she wasn't aware of.

Nora eyed her reflection in the mirror, running her hands along the front of her emerald green dress to brush out a non-existent wrinkle. She hoped the vintage halter dress with its flared skirt and wide belt were appropriate for the day. It was all she had in the color, though, and August had sent her a rather cryptic text the day before telling her to wear green. She hoped the decree didn't extend to Margo because the closest thing she had was a collar with pink peonies and green leaves.

When Rafael showed up promptly at 10 a.m. to pick them up, he was wearing a tan linen suit with a sage green tie.

"You look beautiful." He greeted her.

"So do you," Nora replied, not regretting her choice of words. He really was a beautiful man.

"Thanks." He held a hand out to her. "Shall we?"

"I guess you got the same text from August?" Nora accepted the hand and allowed him to lead her to his SUV.

"I did. This luncheon gets curiouser and curiouser."

"Indeed," Nora agreed. "Mykal thinks August is calling us all together to announce that she's pregnant."

"No way." Rafael shook his head. "I'm not even sure she wants more kids. Leo's career is taking off and now she's got the new show—"

Nora's brow furrowed. "What new show?"

"What?" He was the very picture of innocence.

"Don't play dumb with me, Rafael Medero. You said August had a new show. What new show?"

"Maybe I misheard Leo. I'm sure it's nothing."

Nora didn't believe for one second that it was nothing, but she let it go. As they rounded the last bend in the driveway, the house came into view, and it was clear they were there for more than a luncheon. The entire place looked like a fairy wonderland. Tables were set up with wildflower bouquets and greenery. Wine bottles full of twinkling lights reminiscent of fireflies sat at the center of each one. Strands of lights adorned the trees, peeking merrily through the dripping Spanish moss. Music emanated through the speaker system, a gentle guitar and a crooning voice urging the listener to sway with them.

Nora got out of the car, so enamored with the transformation that it took her a second to realize the canine welcoming committee was absent. "Raf, you don't think—" Nora's words were cut off by an enthusiastic Charlotte racing up to greet them.

"Auntie Nora, Auntie Nora! You're here!"

"I am here." Nora greeted the girl with a hug before standing back to admire her. "And you look so beautiful today!"

The girl preened, fluffing her curls and twirling to show off her dress. "I'm a flower girl! A *fairy* flower girl!"

"My goodness, look at that. You do have wings, don't you?" Nora leaned over to inspect them. "They are lovely."

"Thank you. I asked Mama if you could have wings, too, but she said the maid of honor doesn't get wings. Only the flower girl." Her voice held a hint of apology, like she felt sorry for Nora not having the honor of wings.

"The maid of honor?" Nora repeated.

"Uh-huh. Yep." Charlotte's curls bounced as she nodded. "And Uncle Raf is the best man! But Leo didn't tell me what he was best at."

That proclamation was met with Rafael's deep laugh. Charlotte grabbed each of them by the fingers, and the couple allowed themselves to be led inside, listening to the girl chatter merrily the whole way. By the time she delivered them to Leo, they'd learned that the dogs were in one of the empty animal enclosures for the day so they wouldn't cause any shenanigans. At least that's what Nora thought Charlotte said. She couldn't recreate the girl's pronunciation of the word if she tried.

Leo greeted them with warm hugs. The man was all smiles. Nora couldn't recall ever seeing anyone so happy.

"Were you surprised?" he asked.

"Shocked," Nora admitted.

"Although we shouldn't be," Rafael added. "It's a very August thing to do—a surprise wedding."

"She got tired of all the pressure. Said she just wanted to be married. I agreed, so we put our heads together and threw this together using resources we already had on the property," Leo explained. "Well, we did have to up our wine intake this last week to make the bottle lamps, but that wasn't exactly a hardship."

"Everything looks lovely." Nora meant it. She was impressed at what they were able to accomplish in such a short time.

"Even the flowers came from our fields," Leo informed her proudly.

"They're perfection," Nora said.

"August is in her room getting ready. She'll want to know you're here."

Nora nodded, turning to kiss Rafael on the cheek before excusing herself to find August. She knocked on the bedroom door and waited for August's response before slipping into the room, where she stopped short.

"Oh, sweetheart. You are stunning." Nora couldn't imagine a more perfect wedding dress for her friend. It was a dusty-rose goddess dress that clung to her curves, the layers of the skirt floating around her in a way that truly was magical. Her curls ran wild; a crown of flowers rested on her head. She wore makeup, something Nora wasn't sure she'd ever seen August do. She would have guessed her friend didn't even own any before today. But it was perfectly applied. The colors were subtle, understated, merely accenting her wide eyes, high cheekbones, and full lips.

"Really?" August seemed to blush as she looked down at the dress, smoothing it and twisting a bit to check it from different angles.

"Absolutely. You look like a magical forest spirit."

"I got the dress online. It was $100. I never spend that much on clothing, but it was worth it."

"Every penny and then some," Nora agreed. "Can I do anything to help?"

"Do you think I should try to tame my hair?" August turned to stare at her reflection, a frown creasing her forehead.

"I can twist the sides back for you if you'd like," Nora offered. "But it looks awfully pretty as it is."

"Then we'll leave it. I don't want to have to worry about messing it up. I just want to enjoy the day."

"I think that's wise."

The women smiled at each other for a moment. Nora remembered the moment the wild-haired dog walker blew into her life and found herself overwhelmed with emotion at how far their friendship had come. She wanted to ask if August was leaving her, starting some new adventure without her, but today was not the day. Now was not the time. This moment was August and Leo's and nothing else mattered but them.

"By the way—" August straightened. "Will you be my maid of honor? Sorry for the short notice."

"Charlotte already spilled the beans about ten minutes ago, so I've had plenty of notice. I'd be honored."

August clapped and beamed. "Yay! Here's Leo's ring."

Nora looked down at the ring; it was wood with a vine carved in it and some sort of stone inlay. "It's gorgeous."

"We found them online, too. Had to pay extra to get it in time, but it was still less than anything I saw in town. And it fits us, I think. Mine matches."

"Everything really is perfect." Nora hugged her friend, careful not to mess up her dress. "When is this happening?"

August glanced at the clock. "In about 20 minutes. We asked you and Raf here before anyone else, but the rest of the guests should be here any time now."

"Who's officiating?" Nora asked.

"Rhett!" August informed her with a laugh.

"Rhett Davis?" Nora smiled at the twists life takes. When she'd offered a cup of coffee to the rookie cop assigned to protect her ages ago, she'd never envisioned him one day being the officiant at her best friend's wedding.

"He's a minister through some online church. I remembered it came up in conversation when you were in the hospital, so I reached out and asked if he did weddings."

"How did it come up when I was in the hospital?" Nora wasn't sure she wanted to know.

August shrugged. "I might have asked if anyone knew a minister who could talk to the big guy for us."

"The big guy, as in God?"

She shrugged again. "I'm out of practice and I wanted to be sure we got it right."

"I don't think it works that way but thank you. I appreciate the sentiment."

Before they knew it, there was a knock at the door. Nora wasn't sure who she expected to find, but it definitely wasn't Lucca Buccio.

"I'm here to escort you lovely ladies to the big event," he told her, bowing his head and extending an arm to each of them.

"Why, thank you, kind sir." August gave him a kiss on the cheek before looping her arm through the crook of his elbow. He led them around to the back of the house, where a crowd of twenty or so people gathered under the moss-laden arms of the biggest oak tree Nora had ever seen in her life. All eyes turned to watch them expectantly as they approached. The music that had been playing stopped, replaced by an orchestral piece with lilting violins that Nora was pretty sure was from Litvinovsky's *La forêt et la rivière*. Charlotte skipped down the makeshift aisle, flinging flower petals more than scattering them. When she reached Leo, she turned and waved frantically at Nora. She took that as her cue and started walking, a bouquet of wildflowers in hand.

Halfway down the aisle, Margo appeared, ball in mouth, trying to entreat Nora into a game of fetch. When that failed, she trotted over to Pru, who grabbed the ball and hid it in her pocket. A chuckle rippled through the crowd, silencing when August stepped forward on Lucca's arm.

It all went by in a blur—August floating down the aisle, Lucca giving her away, beaming as if he was her actual father, the short declaration of vows, Leo sweeping her into a kiss, the cheer that went up from the crowd as Rhett introduced Mr. and Mrs. Valfort for the first time.

Just like that, two of her dearest friends were married. Nora dabbed at the tears in her eyes, determined not to look at Rafael. She didn't want him to feel pressured to follow suit. So many men bolted or proposed on the heels of attending weddings. She didn't want anything to upset the delicate balance of their relationship.

The ceremony was beautiful. The reception could only be described as buoyant. Cheerful music piped through the speakers. Friends ate and danced and laughed. There was no regimented schedule, no rules to abide by or hoops to jump through. Just love and laughter and joy. It was the most perfect wedding Nora had ever attended.

When the time came, they all gathered around to send August and Leo off for a brief honeymoon camping up in Alabama. They showered the happy couple with bubbles as they held hands and ran laughing toward their van. Once they were gone, the party down throttled, though several of them lingered on, enjoying the reunion of sorts.

After catching up with Pru and Marcus to hear how the first round of classes went at the new studio, Nora found herself dancing with Raymond. His skill level far outmatched hers, but he was kind enough to not mention that fact as he twirled her around the makeshift floor.

"You are a beautiful dancer," she commented after managing to not fall on her face after a particularly tricky transition. She was certain his skill was the only thing that kept her upright.

"Thank you." He smiled wistfully. "Walter insisted I learn. That man loved to dance."

"I didn't know that." Nora returned his smile. "Sometimes I wonder if I'll ever really know Uncle Walter, if I'll unravel all of the mysteries surrounding him."

"That's the beauty of any relationship, though, isn't it? Getting to know the true person behind the veneer?"

"Yes, I suppose it is." Nora hadn't thought of it like that before, but she could see the truth of his words. "I think I would have liked him, had we met before—"

"I'm certain he would have adored you."

"That makes me happy. I don't know why, but I feel so desperate to know him, to cling to the pieces of him that remain."

"In my many, many years, I have found that something doesn't have to be forever to be important. It doesn't even have to be long term. The transient pieces of our story matter, too. There is no required time threshold to determine merit."

Nora silently absorbed his words.

"It would have made Walter happy to know the *Magnolia Jane* was part of your story, even if it was just a chapter. And it's even okay if there are aspects of him you have to let go of because life isn't one size fits all."

Nora knew he was talking about the *Amelia*, and she knew there was wisdom to his words. She'd gone on an honest-to-goodness treasure hunt because of that boat, a memory she'd cherish for the rest of her life. But she had no desire to run a salvage business, and clinging to it was keeping it from passing on to someone who would love it the way Walter had.

After her dance with Raymond ended, Nora found herself pulling Gregory aside to tell him she'd decided to go through with the sale. He whooped and scooped her into a bear hug, twirling her around before setting her on the ground with a noisy kiss on the forehead and an effusive thank you, leaving Nora to steady herself as he went in search of Ivy. Rafael slipped up behind her, placing a hand at the small of her back in a simple but reassuring gesture.

"I take it you sold him the business?"

"I did."

"Does this mean we're no longer business partners?"

"I kept my share of this find, but the boat and business are his."

"Are you okay?"

Nora paused to examine how she felt. "You know what? I am. Now that it's done, it feels right."

"Good." He kissed her temple. "I do think it was the right thing to do."

His phone chimed and he fished it out of his pocket.

"You didn't turn your phone off? For a wedding?" Nora shook her head reprovingly.

"I forgot. It's not like we had much notice," he defended himself as he checked the text. "But I think you'll forgive me when you see this."

"Is that the logo?" Nora peered at the phone expectantly. What had been a grey blur was now clearly an interlocking U and K. "I know that. I've seen it somewhere before..."

"Yeah?" Rafael looked at her curiously, but Nora didn't respond. She closed her eyes and pressed her fingers to her forehead, as if that would somehow help her think. A moment later, her eyes popped open. Without a word, she headed towards Mykal.

"Hey, Mykal. Do you have your keys on you?"

Confusion flitted across the other woman's face. "They're in my purse."

"Can I see them?"

"Sure. Why? What's up?"

Nora didn't answer, taking the keys from Mykal and holding them up to Rafael. "Recognize the keychain?"

"That can't be a coincidence." Rafael looked from the keychain to Mykal and back again.

"Okay, really. Someone needs to tell me what's so interesting about my keys."

"Remember how I saw something on the surveillance video?" Nora asked. Mykal nodded. "The person was wearing a logo. This logo."

Nora pulled up the video and showed it to Mykal, who watched intently before going white as a sheet and dropping straight to the ground.

Chapter Twelve

ONCE MYKAL HAD BEEN revived from her dead faint, things fell into place rather quickly.

"You know who did it, don't you?" Nora asked after they'd gotten Mykal settled in one of the overstuffed chairs on August's front porch, sipping a glass of water.

"Do you have anything stronger than this?" Mykal handed the water glass to Rafael.

"Sure." He looked from Mykal to Nora for reassurance before heading off to find Mykal a drink.

"We left Kentucky because my mom didn't think I was safe there anymore," Mykal said, her voice soft and stilted. "There was a guy. We were at University of Kentucky together. He was there for the Army. ROTC. We dated for a while. He was so charming. At first."

Nora waited patiently while Mykal collected herself.

"He got weird. Possessive. So, I broke up with him, or I tried to. He started following me everywhere, showing up wherever I was. He was creepy as hell but never came out and threatened me, so the police said they couldn't do anything. It got so bad that Mom decided we should move, start fresh. We came here. I didn't realize at the time, but I think she wanted to be close to Lucca in case we needed protection."

"You think he found you," Nora surmised.

Tears welled up in Mykal's big brown eyes. "The build is the same. The way he moves. Some things you don't forget, no matter how much I wish I could purge him from my memory files forever."

Nora took Mykal's hands in hers. "I am so very sorry."

"I'm the one who's sorry. If it is Brad, then it's my fault you lost your boat."

"If it's Brad, then it's Brad's fault I lost the *Magnolia Jane*, not yours," Nora corrected her gently. "But I'm much more concerned about nearly losing you."

"He must have heard about Edmund." Mykal seemed lost in a distant world somewhere in the recesses of her mind. "I can't imagine why else he'd do something so stupid."

"It's lucky for us Bryan happened along when he did," Nora mused. A thought nibbled at the back of her brain, one she refused to fully acknowledge but couldn't quite ignore. Finally, she asked Mykal, "Do you have a picture of Brad?"

"I'm sure I could find one. Do you have your phone? Mine's in my purse."

Nora refused to spend money on a dress with no pockets, so she did, in fact, have her phone on her. She unlocked it and handed it over to Mykal. A few taps later and Mykal handed the phone back, pointing to the smiling face of their rescuer. "There he is. That's Brad."

"Mykal..." Nora's eyes flew up to meet Mykal's. "That's Bryan."

"I'm pretty sure that's Brad. Look, it says his name right here."

"I know, but I'm telling you that's the man who fished us out of the water. The one who keeps turning up unexpectedly to check on me."

By the time Rafael returned with a glass of Riesling for Mykal, it was to find both women crying and hiccupping and hugging. He took one look at the scene and left, returning a moment later with another glass of wine for Nora, too. She was glad the party had wound down and the happy couple had long since left for their short honeymoon. Otherwise, she's sure they would have made quite the spectacle.

It was bad enough having to explain what was going on to Lucca when he and Charlotte returned from feeding the animals. Nora took Charlotte on a short walk to give Mykal and Lucca space to talk. Even from a distance, she could see the steel settle over Lucca's expression as Mykal recounted her story and knew that didn't bode well for Bryan. Or Brad. Or whatever his name was. Nora watched as Rafael slipped away, from her vantage point, she could see him dialing his phone even as he rounded the corner of the house. If she had to guess, she'd say he was having Rhett or someone he trusted pick Bryan-Brad up before Lucca could put a hit out on him. Or, more likely, kill him with his own two hands.

The next couple of days were a whirlwind. After a bit of a search, Bryan-Brad was found and brought in for questioning. He might have smooth talked his way out of it, had he not come unglued upon seeing Mykal at the station. Knowing who destroyed her boat didn't bring it back, but it did settle the insurance investigation, so that was one thing less to worry about.

When August came to reclaim her daughter, Nora filled her in on the happenings since she'd left.

"Wow. It was the knight in shining cargo shorts all along. What a pity." August shook her head mournfully.

"Does it matter? You're married and I'm in a relationship," Nora reminded her.

"Just in a relationship? Not engaged? I thought for sure being in the wedding would nudge Raf into proposing."

"It did not, but he hasn't run away screaming, either, so there is that."

"Yes, there is that." August sighed, clearly not satisfied with the outcome. "Did Bryan-Brad say why he bothered to save you if he's the one who sank the boat?"

"It seems he had an attack of conscience over killing me, an innocent bystander. Then he pulled Mykal in because he felt bad leaving Terra without even a body to bury. He didn't think she'd live, though."

"What a guy." August's tone was wry. "I'm just glad you figured it out—and that Mykal is safe. Hopefully they'll lock this creep up for a while."

"For his own safety, I hope you're right. If they let him out, Lucca will be waiting."

"Speaking of Lucca—" August hesitated briefly before plunging ahead. "What do you think of hiring him to manage Quirkiosities?"

"Do we need a manager for Quirkiosities?" Nora asked. "Isn't that you?"

"I mean, Lucca did run a successful business. He'd be good to have around."

"I don't know that a crime syndicate counts as a successful business—" Nora hedged.

"It does if it's a successful one," August asserted.

"Okay, but that still doesn't answer my question."

"We both know that Leo let it slip to Rafael that I've been offered a job." August stopped verbally dancing around the heart of the matter. "It's not full-time or anything, it's not that I'd have to leave Quirkiosities altogether, but I'd be gone a lot."

"What about Charlotte?"

"She'd go with me."

"What is this other job?"

"Hosting my own show! Cozy Cryptid Chat." August beamed proudly as she said the name. "Remember when I went with Leo to film that Honey Island Swamp Monster episode? I guess people liked my—" she paused, searching for a word, "—unique approach to the whole thing. The trailer for that episode has done so well that now the production company wants to do a spin-off. Leo's friend Josh will be the frontrunner for Ghosthunters, Inc, and Leo and I will spearhead the cryptid chat.

"Wow." Nora's head was spinning. "That's... a lot. I'm happy for you."

"Are you? Because you look like a kicked puppy."

"I'm just going to miss you."

"I'll still be around. The production company thinks it would be great to tie everything in with Quirkiosities, to make that home base. We'll just be loading Amelia up and going on lots of trips around the country."

"Amelia?" Nora asked.

"The van. The crew named her Amelia."

"Fitting." Nora wasn't sure why, but the name did suit the vehicle, even if it caused a twinge that August's van now shared a name with the boat she'd just sold. She realized she would just have to trust both the *Amelias* to watch over her friends.

August continued her argument, oblivious to the inner dialogue Nora was having over the van's name. "Hiring Lucca would ensure continuity at the farm, and it would give him somewhere safe to lay low. And he and Mykal could maybe build a relationship."

"Okay," Nora acquiesced. "I'll talk to Ivy about it and see what we can do."

"Thank you, thank you, thank you!" August clapped briefly before squeezing Nora in a fierce hug. "Okay, I gotta get back. There's a ton of work to get done before opening day and I have to read up on the Ozark Howler."

"The Ozark Howler?"

"Yeah, our first episode! But don't tell anyone... it's a secret."

"My lips are sealed," Nora promised. "Unless we are going to start building cryptid enclosures. The construction crew may want a heads up on that. And you get to tell Ivy about that one."

As was her custom, August blew out of the house the same way she'd blown in, with all the finesse of a summer storm.

Nora sat back down on her couch, stunned. She was happy for her friend, she truly was, but she couldn't help being afraid of how much things were changing. There was a knock at her door. She thought it might be August having realized she'd forgotten something, but it was Rafael who greeted her when she opened the door.

"I have news," he told her without preamble, giving Nora a quick kiss as he let himself in.

"Okay." Nora was afraid to ask what his news was.

He either missed her hesitation or didn't consider it a deterrent because he cheerfully announced, "I quit my job."

"You quit your job?" She seemed unable to respond to the bombs being dropped on her with anything other than repeating them.

"I did. I've thought about it and thought about it and decided that me being there, trying to clear my family's name years after the fact to people who will never change their minds about me is a waste of time. A waste of my life."

"Oh." It wasn't much, but at least it was something other than a parroted response. She blinked back tears. It wasn't until that exact moment that she realized how much she'd enjoyed trying to solve mysteries with Rafael, however resistant he'd been to her help.

"Nora, mi amor, what's wrong? I thought you'd be happy."

His use of an endearment made the tears she'd been holding back pour freely. "Everything's changing. It just keeps changing."

"Good changes though, right?" he prompted, pulling her into a hug. "This is a good change."

"Pru and her art studio. It was bad enough August moving out to the country, but now she'll be traveling all the time. You're leaving the force. And I'm still just running a bookstore with my dog."

"I know plenty of people who would dearly love to be running a bookstore with their dog, but we both know you'll still find plenty of trouble, even with me changing careers. Your life will never be dull, Nora. And you'll still have me. I'm leaving a job, not you."

"You're right." She straightened and wiped her eyes, embarrassed by the outburst of emotion. "You're right. And I'm being a bad girlfriend. This isn't about me; it's about you. Do you know what you'd like to do next?"

"I was thinking about opening my own agency, being a private investigator."

"That sounds intriguing. Tell me more," Nora encouraged.

"I will, but first I have a question to ask. Nora Jones—" Rafael took her hands in his and looked deeply into her eyes. "Would you open a business with me?"

Nora laughed and pulled Raf in for a kiss. "I thought you'd never ask."

The End

Also by Heather Huffman

Elusive Magic
Some might call it a midlife crisis, but Josie Novak prefers to think of it as a midlife awakening. In this sassy but heartfelt women's romantic fiction, Josie Novak is about to discover that being a woman might not be a fairy tale, but it is an elusive magic all its own.

Elusive Magic is now available at your favorite online bookseller.

The Throwaways
Surprisingly warm and funny, *The Throwaways* are twelve novels that don't shy away from the dark corners of this world but always shine the light of hope. At the core of the series is a group of strong but often unlikely heroes and heroines coming from all walks of life whose lives intertwine as they fight for justice, for love, and to leave their indelible mark on this world.

Immerse yourself in a world of suspense, laughter, and love with *The Throwaways*.

Find Throwaway, book one of this series, at at your favorite online bookseller.

About the author

Heather Huffman writes stories filled with humor, heart, and hope—usually in the form of a cozy mystery or romance. She's lucky enough to be married to her best friend, and the pair is currently working on their own happily ever after in a small town overlooking the Missouri River. When not off on adventure researching the next book, their time is mostly filled with family, their two dogs, a cat who thinks (knows) she's the queen, and a ridiculous number of houseplants. Learn more at heatherhuffman.com.

Author's Note

Wow. This one took a while—sorry about that! The last couple of years have flown by at breakneck speed without a whole lot of writing happening. It's embarrassing how long it took me to get this book out, how many times I pushed back an intended launch. But amid all of the trials and health problems and blah, blah, blah, something crucial happened to me during the silence: I fell in love. I also got married and found myself with the most amazing partner I could ever have asked for. Not only is Justin a great husband and my best friend, but he is also my biggest cheerleader. I don't know if I ever would have finished this book without him. I certainly never thought I'd find myself once again bursting with stories I wanted to tell. I've learned, I hope, to stop making promises when it comes to books, but I will say I'm enjoying writing like I haven't in years and I'm incredibly hopeful that 2025 will be a much more prolific year for me.

I know that life is difficult right now for so many. I sincerely hope this story helped take you away from it for a while, that it put a smile on your face. Thank you for taking the time to read it and for being part of my journey.

xo,
Heather